"Ho, ho, ho?"

T.J. just stared at Nick for several seconds, then she stepped back to let him in the door. He pushed a two-foot Christmas tree at her.

"Find a place for this, will you? By the way, what's for dinner?"

Half an hour later they were seated at the table, eating dinner like two diplomats contemplating a peace treaty. The wine was cool, the chicken tasty and the atmosphere seemed calm and unthreatening. Then Nick started his interrogation. "So, you ever been married?"

T.J. almost choked. Where had *that* come from? "What's it to you?"

Nick put his hands up. "Hey, just asking, all right? I was just wondering if you made a habit of inviting men you hardly know for Christmas dinner. So, I guess there's nobody special in your life right now." He looked perfectly at ease. Only the absolute stillness of his body gave away his interest.

"I'm not a virgin, if that's what you want to know."

"That's definitely a part of it."

T.J. looked at him closely. "Why? What difference does it make?"

Nick took her hand, caressing the palm. "I don't seduce virgins."

Dear Reader,

We all admire men and women who take care of their own. And Officer Nick DeSalvo is definitely one of the good guys, a true Christmas Knight. In order to protect his best friend's wife, he nobly sacrifices his career… and his honor. But it isn't until he meets beautiful T. J. Amberley that Nick realizes just how much his sacrifice is going to cost him.

Nick is a true rebel—with a heart of gold. He's definitely a man you'd want to cuddle with by the fireplace. I hope the sizzling chemistry between Nick and T.J. warms you up no matter how cold it is outdoors.

Merry Christmas,

Lyn Ellis

P.S. Be sure to watch for Jackson's story in *New Year's Knight*, available next month. I had to promise him a book of his own to keep him from arguing with Nick all the way through this one.

CHRISTMAS KNIGHT
Lyn Ellis

Harlequin Books

TORONTO • NEW YORK • LONDON
AMSTERDAM • PARIS • SYDNEY • HAMBURG
STOCKHOLM • ATHENS • TOKYO • MILAN
MADRID • WARSAW • BUDAPEST • AUCKLAND

Okay, Hammer, this one's for you.
Stay warm up there in Buffalo.

And to:

Lt. RMF of the Fulton County Police Department.
Thanks for putting up with a thousand phone calls.
You're definitely one of the good guys.

ISBN 0-373-25715-5

CHRISTMAS KNIGHT

Copyright © 1996 by Gin Ellis.

Printed in U.S.A.

Prologue

"STAY AWAY FROM ME!" The kid brought the gun up higher. Bleeding from a head injury, he'd crawled out of his wrecked car through the broken window and stood with his back to the driver's door, facing the police.

A frisson of pure fear went up Officer Nick De-Salvo's spine. Not fear for himself, but for his friend and partner who was already too close to the teenager. "Gina! Get back." Nick's fingers automatically coiled around the butt of his gun, but he didn't draw it.

"You're okay," Gina said to the scared kid. She had stopped advancing but she didn't retreat. Nick held his breath. "Whatever you're running from can't be that bad," she soothed. "Put the gun down and let's talk."

Tears and blood mingled and made tracks down the boy's face. His eyes were wild and unfocused. "I can't!"

"Gina, he's—" Nick started to protest.

"Stay away from me," the kid said once more, raising the gun to his head.

"Don't do anything stupid!" Gina warned and took another step closer. "Let's talk about it."

Nick couldn't think of a worse scenario. There were no odds in approaching a suspect with a gun. Officer training clearly stated that officers should pull back and wait for backup. This kid wasn't threatening them, but at any second the situation could change.

Even though he knew Gina's personal feelings about suicide, there was no excuse for being reckless with her own life...and his. From the moment Gina had leaped from the patrol car, she'd been breaking every conceivable procedural rule that applied to a scenario like this. He swore under his breath and vowed to strangle her if they got out of this mess alive.

The only thing Nick could think to do was distract the kid. He started walking forward, slowly.

The boy turned his frenzied stare toward him. "I told you to stay away from me." His voice broke as he choked back tears.

"Is there someone we can call for you?" Nick asked, taking another step.

An agonized look crossed the kid's features. "My sister—"

"Okay, what's your sister's name?"

"Tara. She'll..." Suspicion filled his gaze. "No, you'll tell my father." Tears fell in earnest now. He wiped them on his bloody sleeve but held the gun steady. "And he'll have to explain to everybody."

"I'm sure he'll understand." Nick hoped the lie wouldn't be too obvious. Causing an accident and then running from the police, putting any number of people at risk, didn't rank in the realm of *his* understanding. And now, holding them at bay with a gun...

"Put the gun down, son. We aren't going to hurt you."

"No. Not again. I tried so hard but I . . ." His voice faded into a sob.

"We all deserve one more chance. Come on . . ." Nick took another step.

"Not me." The words were flat, without intonation.

A bad sign. Nick didn't need to be a psychologist to detect the sound of defeat. The boy's hand tightened on the weapon, and Gina simultaneously reached for his arm.

The first shot went upward, over the boy's head but Gina was standing between them so Nick couldn't be sure where the next would go. Sprinting forward, he grabbed the boy's other arm and tried to push Gina out of the way. He could smell blood and as he pinned the boy's arm, he could see the terror and determination in his eyes.

Nick thought he must have said something but he didn't hear anything other than the sound of the struggle, the boy's tearful gasp and then another gunshot. For a few seconds the entire scene seemed suspended in time. Then, the gun fired a third time.

Nick blinked up at the sky. That didn't make sense. The kid had punched him and knocked him down. Funny, he would have bet his badge the kid didn't have the strength to accomplish that. Nick tried to sit up, but his right arm wouldn't cooperate. He turned his head.

The teenager had slid down into a sitting position against the car. For the first time he was still. Not fighting, not crying, just still. Gina stood next to him holding his gun. So, she'd gotten it away from him. Good, they could all relax.

"Gina?"

There was no response.

"Gina!" he said again. Why wouldn't she look at him?

When she finally turned to him, he could see tears in her eyes. Something was wrong. Really wrong.

"It's my fault," she said.

"What?" For some reason, Nick was having trouble putting it all together.

"He's dead and it's my fault."

Damn! As the first stabbing pain roared through his shoulder, the truth became obvious. The teenager had carried out his threat, and Nick had been shot. He was more surprised than afraid. He could still think, still breathe. A pang of sympathy for the boy's family registered inside him. But, he couldn't help the kid now. He needed to deal with the living.

Nick ignored his burning shoulder and concentrated on Gina. Words like, *It's my fault* could end a career in a heartbeat. It wasn't anyone's fault that the kid had run from the police, that he'd killed himself rather than face his father. "Stop saying that. It's not your fault," he said, but Gina wasn't listening.

"I thought I could stop him. I thought—"

Nick was starting to feel a little dizzy but he forced himself to focus on Gina. His best buddy's wife. He'd promised Mike he'd look after her and their daughter, Nick's goddaughter. Mike had known he wouldn't be around to protect them.

"Gina," he said. "Look at me. When the sergeant gets here, let me do the talking."

"But I shouldn't have— You're hurt!" She bent over him as she spoke into the radio mike at her shoulder. "Officer down. We need fours and backup. Now!"

"Listen to me," Nick ordered. "You know Mike would want me to handle this, don't you?" It wasn't really fair to push her buttons with what Mike might have wanted, but Nick didn't have time to be fair. A boy had died, technically in the hands of the police. At the very least there would be an inquiry and an internal investigation. Gina had just been forced to relive the past, to remember in vivid detail that her husband had killed himself with his own gun. That was enough.

"You know I can handle this, don't you?" he persisted. "For once, do things my way."

She pressed one hand flat against the wound in his shoulder before meeting his gaze. Then, slowly she nodded.

The ache from the pressure on his shoulder made it hard to breathe. "Good, then don't say anything." His voice sounded strained to his own ears. "When the sergeant gets here, tell him it happened too fast and to ask me."

He watched her for a long moment. He wanted to get up but it hurt too much to try. The red-hot pain in his chest couldn't be cooled by the wetness of the blood soaking his shirt. The sound of sirens was close and insistent. He had to make her agree—out loud, before he could concentrate on his own situation. "Think of Emma, she only has her mother. If you lose your job, what will she have?" More button pushing but he told himself the end justified the means. "What are you going to say when they question you, Gina?"

She brushed away a tear with the back of her hand and took a deep breath. "I'm going to tell them it happened too fast and to ask you."

Nick extended his good hand toward her before she could change her mind.

"Give me the gun."

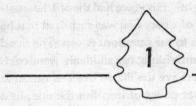

1

THE SURPRISE OF SEEING a car barreling through the crowded city street filled with protesters and the shock of being tackled was wearing off. Tara "T.J." Amberly came up fighting.

"Get off me!" she ordered and pushed a fist into the solid, very human weight that had slammed into her and pinned her to the ground.

Even over the commotion of demonstrators shouting and running, T.J. heard the man holding her down grunt from the impact of her jab. The car that had careened into the crowd had missed her, but what felt like three hundred pounds of Good Samaritan had tackled her midstride.

Male. Her body automatically reacted to his, their intimate position provoking memories she'd been too distracted to sort out. Without warning, a hot flush rose through T.J., reminding her that she was still very much alive and that she'd been alone too long. Slowly, the weight shifted and she looked up into a face—dark eyes, brown or black, a jaw that already seemed to need a shave at eleven o'clock in the morning, and heavy eyebrows, drawn into a severe frown that nearly made her apologize for punching him. Nearly.

"Are you all right?" His voice had the official, matter-of-fact sound of a cop. She was surprised that he didn't add ma'am to the question. A cop. The flood of fluttering warmth filling her suddenly went cold. She'd come to the Save the Planet demonstration to find one particular police officer. But the one she'd been looking for wasn't male. *Don't panic, answer the question.*

Was she all right? Her shoulder hurt like hell. Something metal and unyielding was jammed beneath her. She'd be lucky if the bruise— Then she remembered her equipment and twisted toward the spilled bag next to her. "I will be when you get off me," she grumbled and shoved him again for good measure. She couldn't think coherently with his body sprawled across hers.

The Good Samaritan straightened his arms and pushed up until he was kneeling beside her. The metal rock that had put what felt like a permanent dent in her shoulder turned out to be her new Canon EOS.

"Oh, no." She sat up and gently raised the camera from the asphalt, hoping that appearances could be deceiving. It looked totaled. "Look at this!" She waved the camera in the Good Samaritan's direction. "Ripped the lens right off the mount. Do you know what this thing cost?"

"Lady, that guy almost ran you down with his car. What's your life worth?" The official tone of voice disappeared. Now he sounded like a normal, ticked-off male. Not southern. T.J. had grown up in the suburbs of Atlanta—with southern men. This man's words had a clipped, northern cadence.

She couldn't believe it. He'd tackled her out of the blue, had taken the opportunity to invade her body space from head to toe, and now he looked as if he were waiting for a thank-you. "I was backing up. He would have missed me by six feet. Now, thanks to you, I have a broken lens *and* a broken camera."

"But you don't have a couple of broken legs." The Good Samaritan dusted his hands on his pants then grimaced. When he turned them up, T.J. could see bloody scratches from his sliding tackle on the pavement. He seemed more disgusted than concerned. T.J. again felt that rush of physical awareness, the contradiction of being angry yet wanting to touch him, to take away the hurt. Like she used to kiss away her younger brother's tears when he skinned his knees and elbows. She remained still.

He got to his feet, then glared down at her. His deliberate stare made her nervous. What was he looking for?

"You're welcome—" he cocked his head to read the name tag attached to her camera bag "—Ms.... Amberly." Without offering her a hand up, he stood examining her and if anything, his frown grew darker.

Suddenly the policewoman T.J. had been watching covertly all morning was bent over her. Officer Gina

Tarantino, the woman who had witnessed her brother's death. "Are you hurt? Do you need medical assistance?"

Panic struck. T.J. couldn't look the woman in the eye. Her only plan had been to watch her, to try to decide how to approach her about what had happened that night. T.J. had never intended to be noticed. Well, she'd been noticed all right and now she had to go with it. She pulled her bag closer and stuffed the broken camera inside. "No. I'm fine."

"Nick? Are you okay?" the policewoman asked, but he didn't answer. His attention was on the mayhem before him.

With hands braced on his hips, he looked mad enough to spit. "Look what that butthead did to my building." The beeper on his belt chirped to life.

"Looks like someone wants to talk to the head of security." Gina smiled. "Do you suppose there's been a break-in?"

T.J. turned her full concentration on her Good Samaritan. *Nick.* She slowly rose to her feet. It couldn't be, her mind balked. Her ears rang from the adrenaline rush. Finding and somehow bringing the man who'd shot her brother to justice was to be her only Christmas present this year. For two months she'd studied the case, she'd used the resources at the newspaper, made the basic attempts to find the players. All she'd come up with was Gina Tarantino and she'd pinned her hopes on the policewoman somehow leading her to Nick DeSalvo.

Now the man she'd been determined to see face-to-face stood in front of her. The former cop had become the head of security for Randolf-Reynolds. T.J. had to force herself not to stare.

She looked beyond him toward the beat-up Buick that had swerved through the crowd of demonstrators, shot past them, crossed the sidewalk, and crashed through the marble-and-glass entrance of the Randolf-Reynolds Corporation. And there it sat, at an odd angle, with steam from the radiator rising in the cool December air. One rear wheel was still spinning. The driver was nowhere in sight.

"Did you happen to see the driver?" the policewoman asked.

When the Good Samaritan didn't answer, the policewoman glanced at T.J.

"I didn't see anything," T.J. said quickly, flexing her arm and shoulder to ease the ache. She didn't want to be a documented witness. "The only thing I saw was the color of that unidentified flying person's shirt. I was shooting when he tackled me."

He turned his head and looked directly at her.

"Nick...you of all people...obstructing the press," the policewoman said, amusement clear in her tone.

"Yeah. Imagine that, Gina, me giving a damn about one of the land sharks. If I'd had time to think about it, I would've let her take her chances. All she had to do was photograph him and put his picture on the front page—who needs the police?"

DeSalvo. She knew why she hadn't recognized him right away. He wasn't wearing a uniform or even a suit. And he looked older and angrier than the straight-arrow police officer whose face had been plastered on the front page of the *Atlanta Times Union* and on the evening news two and a half years ago. T.J. felt her face grow warm, but she held his gaze.

When she didn't make a comeback, he seemed to dismiss her. "Was anyone injured?" he asked the policewoman.

"Nothing serious that I've seen. We have a rescue unit on the way...."

Summarily eliminated from importance, T.J. dusted her backside and walked away as nonchalantly as she could on shaky knees.

The impact of looking into ex-Officer Dominick DeSalvo's eyes was just sinking in. *Now that you've found him, what are you going to do?*

She wanted to run. To get as far from him as possible so she could think straight. But she couldn't run, not right now. She needed to go about her job, acting as normal as she could. In case anyone noticed. The newspaper hadn't officially sent her here—she'd come on her own. But she knew how to look as if she belonged.

She pulled her backup camera out of her bag, loaded a new roll of film and started shooting the aftermath of what was supposed to have been a peaceful, environmental demonstration. Before someone's temper got out of control. Where had the car come from? And since when did people get violent over saving the planet? It didn't make sense.

In less than four minutes there seemed to be police everywhere. *Police.* T.J. worked harder. She shot pictures of an injured child sitting on a squad car, a woman holding a broken sign. But the best shot of all was one of a man dressed as Santa Claus helping a limping demonstrator to the medical unit.

One fire rescue truck and two ambulances had arrived to treat the injured, while a gaggle of reporters from the local news stations gathered to film the chaos. No one had been killed but there were plenty of scrapes and bruises, one broken leg, a fractured wrist and what appeared to be a mild heart attack.

Why were these people demonstrating during the holiday season anyway? Didn't they have last minute Christmas shopping to do? Didn't they have families? T.J. would have given anything to be out shopping for a tree, wrapping presents to put under it. Instead, she was on the street, looking for the man who had killed her brother.

T.J. allowed her gaze to run over the scene again, looking for anything she hadn't captured on film.

A familiar blue shirt caught her attention. She spied her Good Samaritan, Nick DeSalvo, standing near the edge of the crowd gathered around the injured, still talking to the uniformed policewoman. He hadn't left town after the investigation into her brother's death as she'd assumed. And he was obviously still in contact with all his old buddies on the police force, especially Officer Tarantino. The ones who'd kept him from going to prison.

The crisp December air sent loose papers tumbling across the street toward him and caused T.J. to pull her jacket closer around her. She raised her camera and studied him through the lens.

He wasn't wearing a jacket and seemed oblivious to the falling temperature, completely involved in serious conversation with the policewoman. A wrecker had arrived to drag the car from the building. Now there was only debris and a gaping hole in the sleek marble-and-tinted glass of the Randolf-Reynolds corporate facade.

Just as T.J. focused on the side of DeSalvo's face, he turned toward her. For a drawn-out moment she stared at his features. Her heart pounded, causing her hands to shake. Her grip tightened. If she was holding a gun instead of a camera ... *Merry Christmas, Officer DeSalvo.* In retaliation, she pushed the shutter button. "Gotcha," she said under her breath, then lowered the camera to meet his stare across the chaos.

His formidable frown returned and for a moment she thought he might march over to her and demand the film. Well, she thought defiantly, he'd have to wrestle her for it. The urge to shoot another picture just to aggravate him ran through her. Instead, because he looked like a man who might be willing to wrestle her, and because she couldn't think of anything else to do, she gave him a challenging, I'm-not-afraid-of-you smile.

Then, as if in warning, she remembered the solid weight of his body, holding her down. Her skin warmed from head to toe. If he was any other man she might have indulged her fantasies. But she *was* afraid of Nick DeSalvo, and there were several very good reasons why she should be. Not enough to make her run, however. Seeing him in the flesh gave her a focus for her anger. She intended to see him put away, along with Gina Tarantino and all the others involved. She was the only one left who knew. The only one who could prove anything.

But not today.

She turned to lose herself in the crowd. Now that she'd found him, she had to decide on a plan. Provoking her target wouldn't help. She knew better than to taunt fate, or an angry policeman. Her brother had faced off with Officer Nick DeSalvo and ended up dead.

NICK DESALVO watched the photographer move away and he shook his head. If he was still in uniform he'd have gone over to hassle her, just for being ungrateful. But what had he expected from an esteemed member of the press? In his opinion, *press* was a four-letter word. He flexed the fingers of his right hand and felt the burn of the pavement again—etched into his bloody palm. He would never have admitted it to her but she'd had a point. The car had been closer to him and might have missed her. But it might not have, and a camera was damned little protection against two tons of Detroit's finest manufacturing.

She walked as if she had somewhere important to go. Determined. His gaze ran over her longish blond hair then moved lower to settle on the sway of her hips. Boyishly dressed in jeans and a Braves team jacket, she blended into the crowd. They usually did, the sneaky ones.

Trying to look tough too, maybe, although the fit of her jeans made him think of supple muscles and smooth skin. She'd felt soft beneath him. He hadn't had time to really savor the sensation, however, before she'd punched him in the stomach. Nothing soft about her knuckles. If he'd registered that she was with the press before he'd tackled her, he might have been ready for the punch.

She'd taken his picture. That made him uneasy. He didn't want anyone digging around in his life again. He needed to be as invisible as possible. A *private* citizen. He'd had enough of seeing his face in the paper or on the six o'clock news. Enough to last a lifetime—

"We're running the vehicle plate," Gina said, bringing him back into the conversation. "Nothing much on the driver. Low in the seat, wearing a dark knit cap—" The radio on her shoulder crackled to life.

Nick listened as the dispatcher informed units on the scene that the suspect's vehicle had been stolen from the parking lot of the Arts Center MARTA train station.

"Well, there's a surprise," Nick drawled not bothering to hide the sarcasm. His attention shifted to the crowd again. He looked from face to face. Sometimes a perp came back to watch. He'd love to get his hands on the creep. "Any description of his clothes?"

"Just dark," Gina answered.

Her radio came to life again. "342. Code 84. Holly and Courtland."

Gina opened the channel. "342. Copy." She looked up at Nick, smiled and shrugged. "Duty calls. Somebody has to work traffic. Let me know about dinner. Your goddaughter would love to see you."

Before he could answer, Gina glanced past his shoulder and frowned. "Look out, incoming idiot. Talk to you later." She placed her hand briefly on the holster at her hip then hitched her gun belt higher before moving away.

Nick heard the voice before he saw the face. "What are you doing here, DeSalvo? Need a little adrenaline fix? Or, did you and Miss America have a date?"

He turned to meet trouble head-on. "Up yours, Butler. It's a free country, or it was the last I heard. But then with upstanding officers like you protecting the city of Atlanta, anything could happen." Before patrolman Butler could respond, Nick made one more jab. "Making a little overtime?"

"Hey, I still have a real career. Not some sissy babysitting job like *corporate security.*"

Being fired from the police department hadn't hurt Nick's reputation in the civilian job market. Randolf-Reynolds had romanced him with all the right perks, the best one being the opportunity to remain in Atlanta so that he could take care of his unfinished business with certain members of the police department. The ones who knew the truth about Mike's death.

Nick almost smiled before dragging out the sharpest weapon he had to cut the conversation short. "I make three times what you make, Butler. At that price I'll baby-sit anybody—even you."

Butler's face turned a dull shade of red and the hand resting near his gun tightened. He drew himself up a little straighter.

"Looks like you have a great big old hole to baby-sit tonight." He seemed to gather steam. "Why didn't you jump out in front of that car like Rambo and stop him? We know you know how to shoot people. Or don't they let you carry a gun? Isn't it part of your job to protect the almighty corporate image?"

"Isn't it your job to find out who did this instead of standing here flapping your gums at me?"

Nick walked away before he lost his temper. Butler wasn't worth it. And there was little he could do to change the man's opinion of him. Even if he'd cared to. Some people believed what they read in the papers—without asking what really happened. It wouldn't do to let Butler find out that Nick would trade anything just to be wearing a uniform again.

T.J. PUNCHED IN the security code for the entrance of her building and waited for the click. After all her painstaking preparations, the day had turned into chaos. She'd gone to the demonstration in the hope of crossing paths with Officer Gina Tarantino. T.J. had done the research, found out what beat Officer Tarantino worked, what shift. But today, not only had they crossed paths, T.J. had literally run into Dominick DeSalvo. Or, he'd run into her. *Saved her life,* or so he believed. If he'd known who she was, he probably would've given her a push in the other direction.

The whole situation was too bizarre to comprehend. T.J. felt as if she were operating on automatic. Her life had just taken a sharp left turn, yet her logic hadn't quite gotten the news. She'd dropped the film by the processor, even the roll from the broken camera, the same as she did every day.

But for once, her dream job of being a photographer for the newspaper didn't matter. The pictures were irrelevant. She didn't need them. Not now. Except maybe the picture of DeSalvo.

Right now, she only wanted to be safe inside. She needed to think, to decide what to do about Officer

Nick DeSalvo and his other friends who were still on the police force.

She swung the door open. The entryway wasn't much warmer than the December wind outside. T.J. glanced up at the beams at least twenty-five feet above her head and knew where most of the heat had gone. She lived in part of a converted factory called the Pegasus Coach Works that had been built shortly before WWI. Now, instead of housing the machinery for building carriages, then later railroad cars, the large facility had been divided by urban architects into two galleries and twenty-five studio lofts.

She crossed the scarred oak floor past the entrance to the Nova Gallery, then stopped at the door that opened to the residential section of the complex and punched in the code again.

She'd been dubious when she'd first heard about the Coach Works. It was in a run-down, industrial part of town backed by a railroad siding. The perfect place for a factory, but not a preferred neighborhood to live in. The outside of the building had remained unchanged except for the new skylights in the roof line and several iron balconies outside upper-level windows. The parking lot sported a new, eight foot high, chain-link fence with razor wire curled menacingly along the top.

But her trepidation had evolved into excitement the moment the inner door to the courtyard had opened. It had been spring when she'd first seen it, a month after her father's funeral, and she'd been determined to find a place to live. A new place, without memories.

As she took in the view again for the hundredth time, she still felt as if she'd come home. Well-placed stepping-stones led downward into a Japanese-style garden, complete with bridge and koi pond. In warmer weather, the walkway wound through flowering shrubs and green, manicured Bermuda grass— a walled oasis between the three factory buildings. The vision remained clear even on this cold fall day. There were pieces of sculpture and wind chimes, several stone benches and even a swing. Everything was tended with loving care and placed with an artist's eye.

T.J. moved down the walk, but kept her eyes on the two things in the courtyard that looked out of place: a huge, black-and-chrome Harley-Davidson motorcycle, and a man, dressed mostly in beat-up leather, with a mane of longish, dark blond hair that any barber would have itched to cut. As she got closer, T.J. could see the stylized chain pattern of the silver bracelet around his left wrist. He looked as if he'd be more at home on a construction site than in this elegant, ordered environment.

The man turned slightly toward her but didn't change his scowling expression. "Hey, T. What's up?" His mouth barely moved.

"Hey, Jackson. Nothing much." *Nothing much . . .* Hysteria coiled inside her. *Nothing except I just met the man who murdered my brother.* She watched as he polished the chrome strut of the bike.

His concentration remained on one particular smudge of grease. "How was the demonstration?"

T.J. searched inside for a normal-sounding voice. She had to clear her throat before she found it. "Great. You should have been there. Somebody ran through the crowd with a car."

"Cool." He looked at her then, before glancing at her equipment bag. "Do we see film at eleven?"

T.J. hitched the bag higher on her shoulder and tried to give him a smile. "Not much to see. Some over-zealous gork knocked me down in the middle of it. He decided he needed to save my life. All he ended up doing was breaking my camera."

Jackson slowly pushed to his feet and his perpetual scowl took a turn for the worse. He wiped his hands on a rag then flexed them in a sinister gesture. "Did you get his name?"

Did she get his name? His concern surprised her. If she'd had to describe Jackson, she would have used words like aloof, arrogant, and antisocial. Talented would have to be included. And striking. His bad-boy persona kept most people at bay—except for the women. Most of them he ignored. God help them all if he ever turned on the charm.

Jackson knew who her father was. They'd discussed family when she'd first moved in and she hadn't bothered to keep her father's name a secret. His father had worked with the county commission at one point and he remembered Commissioner Tilton although he'd never met him or T.J. He didn't know about Rusty.

She'd lived in the Pegasus Coach Works for eight months and most of the time, he'd treated her like an adopted little sister. But now, to have him ready to defend her honor, whether she wanted to be defended or not, nearly brought tears to her eyes.

For a moment, the wild impulse to tell Jackson everything about her father's dilemma and her brother's murder pulled at her. She desperately wished she could talk to someone. To tell someone what she'd kept quiet about for the last two months and what her father had kept secret for the last two and a half years to protect her. To keep her from ending up dead, like her brother. But she couldn't involve Jackson, or anyone else in this. She had to face it on her own.

She blinked and had to swallow hard around the lump in her throat. "No, no name, but I'll point him out if I ever see him again."

Just then a cold gust of air swept around them, setting the wind chimes in a nearby tree into a tinkling melody. The sound seemed melancholy, as if wind chimes and winter didn't go together.

She didn't really want to see Nick DeSalvo again— ever. Unless it was in court.

"Why are you working outside in this cold?" she asked, trying to divert her thoughts and Jackson's attention.

Jackson shrugged and turned back to study the smooth, gleaming chrome of the motorcycle. "I like the cold. Besides, it gives Tyler something to worry about. He thinks I'm going to ruin the landscaping. I make it a point not to bend a precious leaf."

T.J. sighed. She knew about the good-natured, running battle between Tyler, the effeminate building manager—and the star tenant of Pegasus. Jackson Gray—construction welder, steel walker, turned artist. Hometown guy, made good. His huge metal sculptures graced the gardens of museums, courtyards of galleries, and corporate lobbies from New York to Tokyo. Yet to look at him, you'd think he broke legs for a living. Mr. Macho. She felt sorry for poor, proper, anal-retentive Tyler.

"You know, Jackson, he's just doing his job."

Jackson actually smiled, showing perfect teeth, before he caught himself. "Yeah, but I got a problem with people trying to tell me what to do. Always have. And Tyler takes his job a little too seriously. He needs to lighten up."

Shaking her head, T.J. looked toward her door. There was a note fluttering from a piece of tape. Her feet felt like blocks of ice. "Well, I'm going inside where it's warm. See ya later."

"Uh-huh," he said and raised a few fingers of one hand but didn't look at her again.

T.J. followed the stepping-stones to the entrance of her loft. She snatched the note from the glass portion of her door and stuck her key into the dead bolt. A welcoming current of warmth surrounded her as she stepped inside, and with practiced ease, disabled the security system.

Home sweet home.

She didn't miss her family home; there were too many bad memories. Here she had a community courtyard and lots of space. Enough room for her photography equipment and business office downstairs, along with a large kitchen and living room, and a cozy place to sleep, all her own, in the loft above. She even had a trapdoor that opened onto the roof. What more could anyone want?

Safety. She sighed and swung her heavy camera bag onto the counter in the entryway. Would she be safe here when she went after DeSalvo? Was any place safe from the police? Her father must have believed there wasn't.

Now she finally understood why he'd sent her away to college under her mother's maiden name. Why he'd refused to let her confront the man who'd killed her brother. At the time he'd said he didn't want her life to be disrupted by the press and her connection to him as a political figure. But now she knew the real reason.

Her father must have believed that the men who'd killed Rusty would kill her, too, if he came forward with the evidence he had against them: written statements, taped confessions and a gun used in an armed robbery he'd gotten from a policeman, one of the men involved. Shortly afterward, the officer who'd confessed committed suicide leaving justice in her father's hands. Now the evidence and the call for justice had been passed to her.

She stared down at the note the security guard had taped to her door; it was from one of the other stringers at the paper, written on an old cash register receipt.

T.J.—
In the neighborhood, stopped by. The big Kahuna heard you were at the demonstration. If you got anything good, bring it in.

                                                    Lane.

Operating on automatic seemed safe right now. In the two hours it would take for her film to be processed, she could make some phone calls and see about getting her camera fixed. Moving forward. That sounded like the best idea. Until she decided what to do about DeSalvo.

JUST AS she'd expected.

T.J. shoved the last pile of slides into the stack loader; the unfinished roll she'd taken out of the broken camera. Nothing outstanding in her pictures of the demonstration so far. They were just as she remembered, competent but not exceptional. She'd been too busy with her own agenda.

Unless you counted the shot she'd taken of her angry Good Samaritan—Nick DeSalvo. It bordered on the exceptional if only for the hard planes of his face and the implied threat in his direct gaze. The image was unsettling, the look in his eyes made her uneasy. It brought back all the conflicting signals she'd experienced at the demonstration when she'd been lying on the pavement beneath him. On a pure male-female level something about him drew her and that pull fueled her outrage—at herself, and at him.

T.J. chalked it up to having been alone too long. The only thing she wanted from Nick DeSalvo was to see his head on a platter, or more realistically, his face behind bars.

She'd shot the picture even though he obviously hadn't wanted his photo taken. Now, looking at it, she experienced several emotions at once, jumbled between the relief of having gotten away from him in one piece and curiosity about why *he* seemed so bitter. What did he have to be bitter about? He'd literally gotten away with murder.

As she hit the advance button and viewed the first shot on the partial roll, she found herself searching the crowd of people for him. She knew he'd been there, but where? There were a few shots of Gina Tarantino, working the crowd. Two or three frames later, T.J. saw the bumper of a car emerging. The next shot showed part of the hood and several demonstrators scrambling out of the way. The following frame was blurred, she must have gotten bumped. With shaky fingers, she pressed the advance button.

The next slide was sharp. T.J. stopped and stared at the screen. An out-of-focus blur of blue obscured the right-hand corner of the image—her Good Samaritan in action. But to the left of center, in perfect focus, the driver of the car was looking directly at her—frozen forever by the lens of her camera. T.J. drew in a long, slow breath.

Then, she called the *Atlanta Times Union*.

2

FOR SEVERAL LONG seconds Nick stared at the photo on the front page of the *Atlanta Times Union* morning edition. Then, he did something he rarely did. He smiled. After being a front page celebrity himself, he hated the press. But, he had to admit that in cases like this one, maybe the answer to crime and overworked police departments was to give every good citizen a camera and free film.

Looking for the citizen's name, Nick moved his gaze from the perp's distinct features down to the photo credit. The byline read: "Photo by T. J. Amberly." Nick lost his good humor. He flexed his fingers and the pain of the abrasions on his palm reminded him of the lesson he had yet to learn. Helping always hurt.

Amberly. So, she'd gotten her pictures, broken camera and all. And it had only cost him a few strips of skin and a black-and-blue knee. He'd had worse. At least it wasn't *his* face staring back from the front page.

But, as far as he was concerned, it was *his* building the car had smashed. And, he took it personally. Randolf-Reynolds paid him a lot of money to look out for their interests. It had taken Nick most of the day and part of the evening to get the building secured.

He'd had to have the alarm system rerouted and assign extra people for a night watch. He couldn't wait to have a few words with the dirtbag who'd had the misfortune of being caught by Ms. Amberly's camera. He tossed the paper down on his desk and picked up the phone book.

THE PHONE HAD STARTED to ring shortly after 8:00 a.m., and didn't seem to want to stop. T.J. hung up the receiver and turned to face the large, floor-to-ceiling, glass windows overlooking the courtyard.

Even Jackson had stomped across the stepping-stones to congratulate her. And now, looking like a militant mercenary stranded in civilization, he sat slouched on a lawn chair in the middle of Tyler's well-tended grass, contemplating his art, she supposed. He certainly wasn't going to get a tan. They'd had frost two nights earlier.

The buzz of the security door cut through her thoughts. She walked over to the intercom and pushed the answer button.

"Yes?"

"T. J. Amberly?"

"Yes. Who's this?"

"Nick DeSalvo. I—" he paused briefly "—met you yesterday at the demonstration."

"Just a second." Her finger slid off the speaker button as she leaned against the wall. Suddenly, she needed something to hold her up. *Nick DeSalvo.* Her heart pounded with slow hard beats of alarm as she fought panic. She wasn't ready yet.

What was he doing here? He couldn't possibly have recognized her. She and her brother had shared their mother's chin and eye color but there had been no other feature to give away the fact that they were related. She still used her mother's name instead of her father's. But, maybe you always remembered the face of someone you'd killed. She hoped so, because she was going to make damned sure Nick DeSalvo remembered Rusty.

But not today, she wasn't ready. *Pull yourself together. He can't get in unless you let him in.* T.J. took a deep breath and raised one shaking hand to the intercom.

"What do you want?" she asked in the voice she used to get rid of unwanted salesmen.

"I want to talk to you about the photos you took yesterday. May I come in?"

"No," her panic spoke. "I mean . . . I'm a little busy right now."

"I'll wait, then."

She'd hoped he might go away. The thought of him hanging around her building was more unnerving than speaking to him and sending him on his way. She pushed the door release. The intercom buzzed again, then clicked. "...come through the courtyard. I'll meet you."

Better to meet him outside. She looked through the window once more as she pulled on a jacket. Jackson was up and hauling a crate full of metal pipes and sheets of copper.

She opened the door of her loft and stepped out into the cool air.

Nick entered the courtyard and within a couple steps he knew he'd been wrong. When he'd heard the address, The Pegasus Coach Works, he'd had serious doubts about anyone who paid good money to live in one of these drafty, crumbling factory buildings. But now, his doubts were fading.

The factory yard between the buildings had been turned into a protected, private garden. Not unlike the grounds of the exclusive town home complex where he lived. His complex had gates at the entrance and eight foot brick walls with wrought iron rails along the top. It also had a former cop as a resident who paid attention to security.

He glanced toward the far end of the courtyard. The wall between this pleasant place and the not so pleasant outside world was high and substantial. It gave the impression of solid security and privacy. Not such a bad choice. Any security could be breached, by an inventive thief or a determined criminal, and that's where the police came into play. The line between the victim and the victimizer. He'd been both in his illustrious career.

He saw T. J. Amberly before she saw him. He watched her walk across the stones placed in the grass. Her height was the first thing he noticed. On the ground, underneath him, she'd felt small and crushable. On her own two feet she looked capable and able to look any man in the eye. However, now she seemed wary.

And smart. She'd rather stand out in the cold and talk than invite him into her home. Nick glanced beyond her to the man she'd walked over to meet and his own wariness took a leap. Who was the biker? Her boyfriend? Or worse, her husband?

Jackson looked up at T.J. as she approached. "You in some kind of trouble?" he asked.

T.J. turned to face him. Was her fear written all over her face? She stuck her hands in her jacket pockets so he wouldn't see them shaking. "Not that I know of. He's here because of the photo."

Jackson lowered the crate he held to the ground then straightened. "Looks like a cop. I know a lawyer. Want me to call him?" His gaze remained locked on Nick DeSalvo. "You know, when your work gets out into the public eye," he hesitated slightly, then continued, "things can get weird. Believe me, I've been there."

That statement was the most personal revelation Jackson had ever made. He'd talked about her work before but never his own. T.J.'s fear ebbed to reasonable proportions. Nick DeSalvo wasn't going to pull out a gun and shoot her right in the courtyard of her own building with Jackson as a witness. She would just have to play the game. "I can handle it. Besides, I probably can't afford your lawyer," she joked halfheartedly. She drew in a breath and tried to relax. "I guess the first step is to see what he wants."

Nick kept his eyes on T. J. Amberly. He'd wanted to talk to her alone for more reasons than he wanted to admit, but this would have to do.

She spoke first. "Hello." Her voice had a business-like tone, reserved. She blinked and pushed a strand of long blond hair behind her ear.

"*Ms.* Amberly," Nick said as he offered his hand. The smooth warmth of her palm made his feel all the more cold and rough from his skid on the asphalt. After a brief connection, she pulled her hand from his.

"You're a policeman?" she asked.

"No," he said, surprised by the question. No one had accused him of being a policeman in quite a while. No one had the nerve to bring it up. "I'm a concerned citizen. I'm also head of security at Randolf-Reynolds."

The biker moved forward as if he had a right to be included in the conversation. T.J. turned toward him.

"Jackson? This is the gor—" Her gaze met Nick's again for a second. She didn't look particularly friendly. "This is the *concerned citizen* who knocked me down and saved my life yesterday."

Nick found himself pinned by the man's stare. "The one who broke your camera," Jackson added in a menacing voice. In the few seconds of silence that followed, Nick remembered why he always carried a weapon.

He ignored the implied threat and concentrated on T. J. Amberly. "I'm here to talk about the pictures you took. The one that appeared in the paper and any others you may have from the demonstration."

T. J. Amberly brought one hand up to rest lightly on the biker's forearm, as if she meant to protect *him*. "What about them?" she asked. Her wariness had returned. The biker's gaze reluctantly released Nick.

"I'd like to see the rest of the film."

"Why?"

Nick lost his meager amount of calculated charm. "Look, that son of a bitch drove a car through the front entrance of *my* building—"

"Your building?" The incredulous question barely slowed him down.

"—and, in case you've forgotten, he almost flattened you in the process. I intend to have a long, unpleasant conversation with the driver as soon as I find him. Your pictures are the best lead I've got."

"Why don't you let the police handle it?"

Now there was an excellent question. Nick had to pull his anger back under control. "I'm sure you'll be hearing from them, but I work for Randolf-Reynolds. You notice who got here first."

T.J. didn't want to show him anything. She looked from DeSalvo to Jackson trying to decide. "You know I'm protected by the first amendment and I don't have to—"

DeSalvo was already shaking his head. "You don't have to show me anything. I know that. Why don't we call it a favor? Just in case I actually did save your butt on the street yesterday." He let her think about that for a moment. "Maybe I can find him before the police get around to it and you won't have to see a subpoena with your name on it."

A subpoena? The last thing she needed was the police at her door with a search warrant. "All right, I'll show you the film."

Both Jackson and DeSalvo looked surprised by her answer.

"You don't have to do this—" Jackson began.

"I know." She tried to give him a reassuring, unafraid smile but her mouth felt stiff. She shifted her attention to DeSalvo. "Let's get it over with."

"T.J.—" Jackson stopped them.

"It's all right, Jackson. It'll only take a few minutes."

"Well, I'll be out here working," Jackson said. "If you need me . . ." his hostility radiated in the cool air ". . . yell."

T.J. walked away from Jackson with some regret. She could handle her own problems but it was nice to have some solid, uncomplicated physical support. Especially when the mere act of looking into Nick DeSalvo's dark, angry eyes seemed to freeze her thinking processes. There was no friendliness in his expression, only frank assessment. As if he had the right to stare through her skin and study her thoughts. Her motives. This man treated the world as if at any second it might coil up and strike at him. And Jackson had nearly done just that.

If DeSalvo had been wearing a suit or even a uniform, she might have dealt with him better. She'd grown up around men in suits: lawyers like her father, politicians, government workers. Even the policeman who would occasionally drive her father around when he was a county commissioner had worn a suit.

DeSalvo wore khaki pants and a tweedy-looking sport jacket. He looked comfortable and casual and attractive unless you noticed the implacable set of his jaw. Or looked into his eyes.

T.J. swung open the door of her loft. Without giving DeSalvo any time to scrutinize his surroundings, she moved toward the hallway and the small room she used for slide storage and projection. The slides from the day before were still in stacks on the light box. "This way."

T.J. closed the door of the projection room after them and immediately decided the dimensions were too small. She didn't want to be close to Nick De-Salvo. As they stood shoulder to shoulder in the dark, T.J. cued the projector to show slide after slide and reminded herself to breathe.

When the screen filled with his own angry face, Nick turned to look at T.J. Even in the dark she looked uncomfortable and he would bet his next paycheck she was blushing. What did that mean? Her finger quickly jabbed the advance button. Soon they reached the last roll.

"This is the sequence of the crime," she said and pushed the button. Instead of the driver in the car however, the first three photos were of Gina Tarantino. Ms. Amberly speeded her progress through them until she reached the first picture with the car.

There was no discussion. After the last slide, T.J. flicked on the lights. She looked even more nervous than she had outside. She suddenly became more helpful.

"The newspaper has the best frame of the driver— the one they used for the story. I'll have copies made of these and send them over to you."

"Why were you so interested in the police officers who were at the demonstration?" He had to ask, just to see how Ms. Nervousness would answer.

The color promptly drained out of her face. "What? I mean...I shoot everything. You never know how the story will be written and—"

"Newspapers don't run stories about cops unless it's bad news."

She seemed to draw herself together at that. "Hey, she's a woman, I'm a woman. We're both doing a tough job. Besides, I can shoot pictures of anything or anyone on the street. It's a free—"

"—country. Yeah, I know that speech. I've lived through the perils of protecting it." He decided to let her off the hook, for now. "Thank you for showing me the film. I would like copies. Maybe I can come up with more witnesses, someone who connects to the perpetrator. And send a bill with them—the corporation will pay it."

T.J. opened the door and waited for him to precede her. The small slide room was a really bad place for a confrontation. She felt trapped already and when he moved past her, close enough to brush her clothes as he went by, she felt physically overwhelmed. She couldn't trust her voice not to betray those feelings. T.J. wanted to get Nick DeSalvo out of her loft before he could ask any more questions. Because she was such a bad liar that she might slip up and tell him the truth.

She couldn't believe she'd forgotten about the pictures of Gina Tarantino. Then when he'd confronted her about it, she'd realized how far out of her depth she was. The man put two and two together before she realized she'd presented the equation.

He took his time moving down the hallway, stopping at each framed piece of her work displayed on the white wall. He stopped in front of a black-and-white portrait she'd taken of Jackson on his Harley with one of his friends, Rita, draped dramatically across the back of the leather seat. Intimacy was part of art but somehow watching Nick DeSalvo study the print embarrassed her. T.J. shifted on her feet wanting to pull him away. At least Jackson had his jeans on while Rita had gone for the long, lean, spandex-leopard-skin bodysuit look.

T.J. refused to apologize for the shot. Jackson's hard-planed masculinity accentuated by the cool chrome and metal of his motorcycle was the perfect foil for Rita's smooth grace. What would an ex-cop know about art, anyway?

Finally, without making a comment, DeSalvo moved. As she ushered him along toward the front door feeling relieved, the intercom buzzed. She couldn't open the front door and answer the caller at the same time.

DeSalvo paused near the counter along the wall of the entryway where her broken camera rested like an avant-garde piece of Jackson's sculpture.

"Yes?" She answered the intercom without taking her eyes off him.

"Atlanta police, ma'am. I need to speak to T. J. Amberly."

DeSalvo looked at her and shrugged as if to say, *I told you so*. But he didn't seem pleased.

T.J. fleetingly thought of Jackson and his lawyer. She might need him after all. She gave the detective instructions to her loft then buzzed the door open.

"I'd appreciate it if you'd get copies made for me before you give the film to the department," DeSalvo said.

"Why would I give them the film?"

"Because that's what he's here for. He probably doesn't have a subpoena yet, so you could put him off for a day or so."

T.J. wondered why he was telling her this. And she also wondered why he made it sound as if the department was his adversary. He was one of them. *We all bleed blue.*

DeSalvo opened the front door for the detective.

The detective looked surprised. "What in the—" He glanced toward T.J., then returned his attention to DeSalvo. "What are you doing here?"

"Hi, Bill, it's been awhile." The two men shook hands, and T.J. wanted to scream, then push them both out the door and lock it after them.

"I was just on my way out," DeSalvo said without answering the detective's question. "Do me a favor and don't mention me to the lieutenant."

"I may be crazy, but I'm not stupid. Echols finds out you were here and I get the week from hell."

"Yeah." Nick awarded him a smile that held no humor. "See ya later." He turned to T.J. "I appreciate your help, Ms. Amberly," he said. His voice sounded official, but his eyes held a warning.

After the front door to the loft closed behind him, Nick stopped outside to regroup. He was glad for the cooler air. It helped get his mind off the unexpected physical reaction he'd had to T. J. Amberly when she'd faced him down. He'd wanted to touch her, to challenge her with his mouth and provoke her with his hands. To see just how she would choose to handle him—one-on-one. He needed to get his mind back to business.

He figured she could handle Detective Bill Raymond. Bill was the real thing—one of the good guys. He wouldn't step over the line. But why was he even worried about her? She hadn't been particularly friendly to him, and her anger about him knocking her down seemed way out of proportion.

Maybe she didn't like men, he thought uncharitably. Or, maybe she only liked a certain kind of man. Nick looked across the courtyard and there, lounging on a lawn chair in the cool December sun, sat the biker.

Instead of using the stepping-stones, Nick cut directly across the winter-browned grass.

He took in the attitude, the leather and the lack of a haircut. Most of these guys were the same—the proverbial shallow end of the evolutionary pool—antisocial behavior and high testosterone. This one looked at least thirty, past the age of being a punk and into the realm of dangerous. He had size and an I-don't-give-a-shit look in his eyes. But there was something else, something calculating that made Nick curious. This guy's pool might be a little deeper.

Nick stopped a few feet from the lawn chair and shoved his hands in his pockets. "You live here?"

The biker just stared at him. Then he shifted position to put his arms behind his head, keeping his hands in sight like he knew the drill. "If I did, I'd tell you that the building manager gets ticked when people walk on his grass."

"You're on the grass."

"I pay for the privilege."

"You got a last name?"

"You got a reason for askin'?"

"Maybe I want to put it into a computer. See if you have any warrants."

The biker's mouth twisted into a smirk. "Hey, you don't scare me. My old man was a cop, and I'm not wanted for anything . . . but my art."

"What's your relationship to Ms. Amberly?"

The smirk disappeared and the arms came down to rest on the chair. The attitude shifted into the red zone. "I'm her friggin' guardian angel." He slowly pushed to his feet. "What's it to you?"

Nick removed his hands from his pockets and widened his stance. He'd wanted to provoke him and he'd gotten his wish. He was in just the right mood to go a few rounds. Besides, something inside Nick needed to push, to find out if this guy knew what was behind all those white doors in T. J. Amberly's loft. Like which one was her bedroom.

"Jackson?" T.J.'s voice reached them across the courtyard.

Nick held the biker's gaze, waiting.

"Yeah?" Jackson answered without looking in her direction.

"I need to talk to you."

Need. The word scraped along Nick's nerves. He didn't like the sound of that.

"Be right there . . . *hon.*" The smirk returned. "Gotta go, man," Jackson said with a shrug and brushed by him. "You know the way out."

Nick watched as the biker clumped over the step-ping-stones to T. J. Amberly's door and felt the un-reasonable urge to follow him. But, as a civilian, there was only so much room to push, and he'd just met the wall.

3

BY MIDNIGHT, she'd had at least fifty phone calls. The first forty had been business or friends, the last ten turned out to be hang-ups. The phone rang again and T.J. picked it up.

"Hello?"

Silence.

"Hello? Who is this?"

Still no answer.

"Do you know what time it is?" T.J. asked in exasperation.

The line went dead. Another hang-up. But this time they'd waited for her to speak. She slowly put the receiver down. She wished she hadn't answered it in the first place. Now she had to worry about what it might mean. Had some weirdo picked out her number and decided to harass her?

Harassment. She thought of the police, of Nick DeSalvo. Now there was a bully if she'd ever met one. Physically, anyway. She remembered the heavy solid weight of him when he'd tackled her. And, she remembered how just his presence in her loft had been intimidating. He'd even tried to intimidate Jackson. Would he call her and hang up? He seemed more like the type who'd say exactly what he wanted to say—in person.

She tipped up the phone and unplugged it. No matter. She wasn't dealing with any more bullies. She'd had enough for one day.

"DON'T YOU EVER answer your phone?" The woman sounded annoyed.

"Excuse me?" T.J. answered, taken aback by the abrupt tone of the caller.

"I've been calling since eight this morning and I—"

"Oh, I'm sorry. I had so many calls yesterday that I unplugged the phone last night. I forgot to—"

"Is this T. J. Amberly, the photographer?"

"Yes. What can I do for you?"

"This is Linda Fredrickson from the Randolf-Reynolds Corporation. I want to talk to you about doing some photography work for us."

The Randolf-Reynolds Corporation. "What did you say?" T.J. had to ask. She'd heard the woman but her comprehension had stopped at the company name.

"Would you be available to do a shoot tomorrow morning? We have an awards breakfast set up and our regular photographer has a conflict."

"Tomorrow? I don't think... Could I ask where you got my name?"

"From our head of security, Nick DeSalvo. He said you were a good photographer and that we should give you a try."

Nick DeSalvo.

He had to know something. T.J. felt another hard rush of doubt. Nick DeSalvo and his friends on the force had covered up the real reason her brother had died, and the police had termed it an accidental shooting. How did she think she could face off with him and the police department all alone and uncover the truth? *Because I have the evidence—a motive for the use of excessive force.*

DeSalvo couldn't possibly know that. And this chance to get close to him wasn't likely to come up again. Let him watch her and wonder. She'd do the same. She could only hope she'd find her opportunity to expose him before he found out her real name and realized that she intended to turn his comfortable life inside out.

T.J. snatched up a pad lying near the phone and uncapped a pen to write down the woman's name. "Sure. I'm available. What do you need? Color or black and white?"

Ms. Fredrickson went on to explain exactly how she expected to use the photographs, and T.J. jotted down a page of notes. They discussed price, contacts and delivery time frame and through the entire conversation, T.J. kept picturing the look on Nick DeSalvo's face when he realized he had helped hire the woman who was going to bring him down.

"NOW, TELL ME again who this woman is?" Lieutenant Echols asked.

Just then, one of the Hawks defense scored after a steal and the crowd went wild. The patrolman had to raise his voice to be heard. "T. J. Amberly. She's a photographer. I checked her out. She's been stringing part-time for the paper about six months. Her résumé said she came straight out of a school in Kentucky."

The men paused in their conversation to let a woman squeeze by their seats on her way to the concession stand. "She lives west of downtown in one of those old factories," the patrolman continued.

"What does that have to do with DeSalvo?" the lieutenant asked.

"Nothing and that's what worries me. This is the first time her name has come up. But according to Butler, DeSalvo seems real interested in her. He's been asking around. He was at her place when Bill Raymond went to question her."

A player on the court missed an easy shot. "Oh, man!" the lieutenant shouted as he pushed to his feet. "You hit that shot in practice with your eyes closed!" The buzzer sounded, signaling the final time period of the basketball game. A referee blew his whistle and raised one arm. The lieutenant took his gaze from the court and pinned the patrolman with a stare. "Maybe you better find out what's so interesting about her."

The crowd roared again, cheering a three pointer. The patrolman nodded and had to yell to be heard. "You got it."

NICK LOOSENED his tie as he paced through the lobby of the Randolf-Reynolds building two days later. He'd finally gotten the out-of-town corporate brass who'd come in for a series of special meetings on a jet and outward-bound. Now he could get back to regular business . . . and he could get rid of the dark blue suit he'd been required to wear. First, the tie.

He waved to the guard at the desk then turned left toward the elevators. As he rounded the corner he nearly ran over T. J. Amberly.

Nick stepped back quickly. Before she could speak, he decided to head her off at the pass. He raised one hand in placation. "Sorry. You don't have to worry, I won't knock you down again." She stood absolutely still staring at him. That's when he noticed that her eyes were bluish green. She still didn't look friendly. He glanced toward the elevator call button but she'd already pushed up.

"Nice suit," she said.

He put his hands on his hips and faced her. What the hell was that supposed to mean? This suit had cost more than his bulletproof vest. His gaze slid from her face to her feet, taking in the change in her attire, searching for ammunition in case he needed a comeback. He hoped he wouldn't since she looked damned good in the suit she was wearing. Businesslike but with softer lines than a man's and in some sort of smoky blue color.

"Thank you. I could say the same about yours." *If I didn't think you'd toss it right back at me*, he thought in irritation then waited for the volley.

Just then the elevator dinged and the doors opened. Nick held the door and gestured for her to precede him.

T.J. entered the empty elevator wondering about God's sense of humor. Of all the people she could list that she wouldn't want to be trapped in an elevator with, her Good Samaritan—Nick DeSalvo—would be number one. T.J. looked at his reflection in the mirrored rear wall of the elevator car and he looked back.

"What floor?" he asked as she turned around.

"Eighteen."

She watched as he pushed the button. He had nice hands, long blunt fingers with just a dusting of hair on the knuckles. She remembered the bloody scratches on them the day he'd tackled her at the demonstration. Then she remembered that his hand had held the gun that killed her brother. A shiver ran through her.

She'd known she would run into him sooner or later and had chosen several things to say to him. But being closed inside the confines of an elevator made the words stick in her throat. He seemed taller than she remembered, and the severity of his tailored suit defined authority. In a uniform he probably looked like the Terminator. She clutched the large brown envelope she was holding a little closer and took a deep breath. She could do this.

"Thank you for the recommendation," she managed to mumble.

His dark gaze dropped to the envelope in her hands and he seemed to relax slightly. "How did it go?"

"Great. That's why I'm here. I'm delivering the finished shots to Linda." Good start. Her voice sounded normal. The words were those of anyone who'd been recommended for a job.

He crossed his arms. "So, did you make enough to pay for the broken camera?"

Understanding rolled over T.J. The recommendation had been an apology, a way to fix what had upset her the most, her broken camera. As if he'd known that a job was the only thing she'd willingly accept from him. T.J. looked into his eyes and reminded herself that this man was her enemy. He hadn't given her brother a chance. She had no need to confess her intentions. Or, feel grateful. "Yes, thank you."

"We're even, then?"

"Not quite," she answered. *Not in this lifetime.*

He looked puzzled, and T.J. regretted her words. It was dangerous to put questions in DeSalvo's naturally suspicious mind.

The elevator reached the eighteenth floor and the doors opened. T.J. stepped out into the corridor.

"Have you had lunch yet?" she continued as if that's what she meant by not being even.

"No."

"You want to?" T.J. did her best to look business-like and...friendly. She didn't want him to think that lunch *meant* anything, other than an apology and a business contact. "I'll buy."

He ran a hand along the back of his neck in a harried gesture. "I could handle that. I haven't had anything but coffee today."

It was not the reaction T.J. had expected. She'd halfway feared that he'd come up with some smart, macho remark about allowing a woman to buy him lunch. Instead, he'd admitted he was hungry. "Um...I have to deliver these shots and speak to Linda briefly, then I can go. Where do I find you?"

"My office is down the hall to the right." He moved in that direction. "Name is on the door," he added. With a wave, he walked away.

THE TIE WAS GONE. That was the first thing T.J. noticed when she saw Nick again. She wondered if he'd left it in his office or had rolled it up and stuck it in his pocket like her dad used to do. Commissioner John Tilton had always been in search of his favorite ties. The memory of her father toughened her resolve. What had he gone through trying to protect her and Rusty? And he'd never said a word.

Asking Nick DeSalvo to lunch had been easy. Going to lunch with him might be a little more difficult. Standing next to him in the elevator again, she suddenly had nothing pleasant or neutral to say. She wanted to turn, put her hands around his throat and scream at him.

Her silence didn't seem to bother Nick. He got right to the point. "What have you decided to do about the photographs of the perp at the demonstration?"

T.J. took a moment to gather her words. He didn't sound angry, only curious. The elevator doors opened and she stepped out before she answered. "The copies you wanted are probably sitting on a counter somewhere in your mail room. I also sent Detective Raymond copies of everything I had...." She couldn't resist adding, "...including the photo of you. The newspaper still has the original of the shot that ran on the front page."

Nick stopped at the revolving door and turned. "Why did you send the picture of me?"

"You were there."

He frowned, but she pushed through the door before he could reply.

He caught up with her on the street and indicated a direction. "This way." His jaw still looked tight. He hadn't mentioned where they were going for lunch and didn't appear to be in the mood to discuss it.

"What's the problem with sending your picture?"

"It's a long story—too long to get into now." He changed the subject. "Ever been to the Peachtree Grill?"

"No, but I've heard of it."

"It's only a few blocks down, next to the Ritz Carlton. Is that okay for lunch?"

"Sure." T.J. pulled her jacket a little closer. The day was bright but windy, and downtown always felt chillier because the buildings blocked the sun. The stores were decorated with twinkling, snowy window scenes to promote the Christmas season and the sidewalks were crowded with shoppers. On the corner, a costumed Santa Claus rang a bell and collected donations for the local food bank.

Surrounded by people, T.J. felt vulnerable again. And alone. She missed both her father and Rusty desperately. She'd be home for Christmas this year. In her hometown that, on the surface, looked friendly and festive, but had become a city full of people she couldn't trust. Especially the man walking next to her. *Merry Christmas. Ho, ho, ho.*

"You cold?" He seemed surprised, as if the idea were ludicrous.

"No. Walking will warm me up."

He gave her a long look, then increased the pace of his steps.

THEY'D BEEN STANDING outside the Peachtree Grill fifteen minutes, waiting for a table, when the shots were fired.

One moment T.J. had been explaining to Nick the process of photographing executives at a meeting, the next moment the window at their backs had exploded into a waterfall of broken glass. A few seconds after that, she'd been squashed face-to-face, head to toe, up against a brick wall by her Good Samaritan—Nick DeSalvo.

4

DeSalvo was warm and solid, and he smelled of laundry soap. T.J. had ended up with her face pressed into the open collar of his shirt—literally breathing down his neck. She turned her face away from the other more intimate scents of after-shave and warm, male skin.

And saw the gun in his hand.

"Are you all right?" He exhaled the question next to her ear but he didn't move.

"Yes," she answered and pushed her hands into his chest. Suddenly she couldn't breathe. "Let me—"

"Wait," he ordered and pressed into her harder to keep her immobile.

The next thirty seconds seemed like a lifetime to T.J. Her mind was in shock but her body went into overload. She wasn't cold anymore. Heat stung her cheeks and ignited under her skin. Bewildered by her body's sensual reaction to this particular man, T.J. could only think of getting away. But he held her firmly trapped. Squirming would be even worse than standing still. Yet how could she just stand there when each breath he took caused his chest to press against her breasts? She was sure he could feel every thump of her pounding heart. *Remember who this man is.*

She concentrated on the gun. She'd seen one like it before. Lighter than the bulky revolvers the police used to carry. Some kind of automatic.

The silence of ear-ringing shock gave way to the rising level of noise around them. Several people were gathered near the entrance of the restaurant, all speaking at once. A siren wailed in the distance.

DeSalvo stepped back from the excruciatingly intimate position but kept T.J.'s back to the wall with one hand clamped on her shoulder, as if she might fall down without his support. His shoes crunched on the glass lying around them but he didn't seem to notice. Holding the gun high, his gaze swept the opposite sidewalk and the cars that had stopped on the street.

As her mental functions returned, T.J. realized she'd dropped her purse. For some inane reason it seemed very important for her to pick it up. She tried to move but DeSalvo's hand tightened on her shoulder. When he finally made eye contact with her, she drew in a quick breath. He looked furious.

"My purse—" Her voice faltered in the face of his anger.

Without a word, he released her shoulder and bent to retrieve her purse with his left hand. After giving it to her, he turned his back yet kept her close to the wall with his mere proximity.

Nick slipped his gun back into the shoulder holster when the first police cruiser arrived. Whoever fired the shots was long gone and wouldn't be back. No need to wave a weapon around. He nodded to one of the officers he knew . . . Washington . . . but couldn't remember his first name.

He glanced at T. J. Amberly. She looked stoic yet pale. As he watched, she nervously brought one hand up to push a strand of hair behind her ear. That's when he noticed how badly her hands were shaking. Nick moved closer and took her arm in case she couldn't move on her own.

"Come on," he said tugging her forward. "Let's wait inside where it's a little warmer."

She didn't argue. In fact she didn't look capable of speech and for some reason that made Nick feel even more homicidal toward whoever fired the shots.

The restaurant was in an uproar about the broken window and the bullet hole in the far wall. Most of the people near the front door had left their tables and were milling around waiting to talk to the police. Some patrons were less concerned and sat finishing their lunches. Nick managed to find the fluttery maître d' and soon he and T.J. were seated in a small booth toward the back—as far as possible from the broken window.

"Are you sure you're okay?" he asked again after he'd ordered coffee and sandwiches for them both. At least the kitchen was still running normally.

"Yes," she answered. "I just feel so odd."

"Being shot at can wreck the whole day," Nick said trying to lighten the situation.

Instead of smiling, she looked at him as if he'd just confessed to being an ax murderer. The icy expression in her eyes didn't look like fear.

"I suppose," she answered noncommittally, looking away.

I suppose? Nick felt as if he'd just had a door slammed in his face. What the— "Why do you *suppose* someone was shooting at us?"

That brought her back to the conversation. "What do you mean, shooting at *us?*" she asked defensively.

He watched her. "Two shots were fired. We were standing in front of that window..." He shrugged. "What did you say you do for a living?"

"You know I'm a photographer. I—"

"Made anybody mad lately?"

Before she could answer, the waiter arrived with their coffee.

As T.J. ripped open the sugar packets with stiff, shaky fingers she said, "I haven't been in town long enough to make any enemies." Her green gaze met his in a challenge. "How about you?"

Nick took a sip of the black coffee and stared at the woman before him. He knew she was lying, but beyond that, *she* looked angry with *him* and he didn't get it. Why? "You know this is the second time I've had to save your butt in a week and you're acting like I'm the bad guy."

"Maybe I don't need to be saved. Maybe I should just stay away from you and I'll be safe."

For some unaccountable reason, Nick's memory flicked back to the sensation of covering her body with his as he'd pressed her into the wall. He hadn't had time to enjoy it then because he'd halfway expected to catch a bullet. But now that they were safe, the feel of her fitted to him seemed imprinted in his skin. He didn't want her to stay away. But he did want her safe.

"We'll eat lunch, talk to the police, then I'll get you back to your place. You'll be safe enough there."

T.J. OPENED the inner door of the Coach Works with Nick DeSalvo standing silently at her back. He'd forced her to eat lunch, intercepted and interpreted questions from the police, and now he was insisting on checking the security of her building and loft.

He wouldn't take no for an answer.

As they traversed the length of the courtyard, T.J. had bypassed the limits of her patience and was clinging to the ragged ends of her sanity. *Be careful what you wish for,* she thought snidely to herself. She'd wished to find Nick DeSalvo and, like magic, he'd practically taken over her life.

"Don't you have a job to get back to?" she asked peevishly, hoping she could make him angry enough to go away and let her regroup.

He didn't answer.

They reached the front door of T.J.'s loft and she turned to face him. "This really isn't necessary. I—"

"What is it about me that makes you so nervous?" He stood there staring at her, daring her to tell him the truth.

T.J. flinched inwardly but held his gaze without blinking. He probably assumed the cause was nothing more than the natural reaction of a skittish female in his manly presence. The satisfaction of disabusing that notion wasn't worth putting her life in imminent danger. *Well, there is the issue of you having killed my brother....* "I don't need your help," she said, ignoring his question.

"Really? You're used to dodging cars and bullets, then? What do you plan to do if someone tries to get in here? Just say no?"

T.J. ignored his sarcasm, but a new thought occurred to her. What if DeSalvo wanted to check out her loft so that *he* could break in? She looked into his eyes. "Why would someone want to break in here?"

"You tell me." His gaze held hers steadily but not in a threatening way.

"Listen." T.J. sighed. Her fears were getting the best of her. Nick DeSalvo had no idea about the sealed briefcase that was hidden in her loft or how the contents of that case would affect his life. He couldn't know—he was just bullying her because he bullied everybody. "I appreciate your concern.... But like I told the police, I don't have any ex-boyfriends hunting me down and I don't make drug deals and I—"

"Just let me check out the windows and doors to this place and I'll leave." When she didn't acquiesce he added, "It's what I do, okay?"

The next twenty minutes may have truly been the longest twenty minutes of T.J.'s life—excluding the funerals for her brother and her father. Nick DeSalvo methodically checked each of the wire mesh covered windows that faced the parking lot. He fooled with the front door latch and dead bolt then tested the alarm system.

Then he climbed the stairs to her sleeping loft.

Facing any man across the expanse of her own haphazardly made bed would have made T.J. nervous. But facing Nick DeSalvo brought back the memory of being squashed between his body and the wall and the embarrassing, spontaneous reaction it caused inside her. She'd been afraid, yet her body had recognized and responded to his solid warm maleness. Her body had no use for logic or grief. Her heart, on the other hand, had had to deal with too much of both. The idea that any part of her might be attracted to Nick DeSalvo made her want to cry. This was the man who had killed her brother. This was the man she'd sworn to destroy.

And he stood there scowling at her. "How do you expect to get out of here if there's a fire?" he asked.

Looking past him, T.J.'s breath caught. There were three photos arranged on her dresser. Two of them were pictures of her father and her brother, Rusty. T.J. worked to find her voice. "The roof." She pointed to the stairs that led up to the trapdoor. "The building is up to code. If you don't believe me, you can talk to the manager."

T.J. casually walked to the dresser and quickly re-arranged the frames facedown as Nick went up the stairs to flip the latch. The door swung outward like a window. He turned to give her a severe look. For a heart-pounding moment, she thought he'd caught her concealing the pictures.

"You don't keep this locked?"

Resisting the urge to give him a hard push through the trapdoor, T.J. left the dresser and followed him up the stairs. "Step out there and then tell me why you think I need to keep it locked."

"Nice view," he said as T.J. joined him on the roof-top balcony.

T.J. looked out over the familiar Atlanta skyline in the distance then she faced Nick DeSalvo. "Yes, I like it." She indicated the steep angles of the roof all around them. "Now do you see why I don't lock the door? Someone would have to be suicidal to try to get into the building this way."

"Not suicidal, just not afraid of heights. Is the door wired into the alarm system?"

"Yes, the—" T.J.'s beeper on her belt interrupted her. She pulled it free and looked at the number on the display. "Well, maybe you don't have to work this af-ternoon, but it looks like I do. I need to call the paper. Have you seen what you wanted to see?"

He nodded. "After you."

Nick followed T.J. down the stairs into her bedroom doing his best to keep his attention away from her bed. The rumpled pillows piled at one end and the fluffy down comforter looked too comfortable, too inviting. It was the kind of bed that made him think of wild, tangled Saturday nights and long, lazy Sunday mornings—lying next to a woman like T. J. Amberly.

She didn't pause, but led him unerringly to the front door, as if she couldn't wait to get rid of him. What had he expected? Welcome? From the first time he'd laid eyes on her, she had been pushing him away, both figuratively and literally. Maybe that's why he couldn't let it go. Police officers were paid to be nosy; it was part of the job.

She was afraid. He could feel it in her—something had her on the run and the old habit of nosing around in people's lives reasserted itself. But he knew better than to get involved. Every time he stepped in front of someone, he was usually the one who got run down for it. And he knew T.J. didn't want *his* help. Well, hell . . . he was the only one around at the moment. Except for the biker.

With one hand on the doorknob he glanced out into the courtyard. "Where's your buddy, the biker?"

"You mean Jackson? He's not really a biker . . . although he does have a motorcycle." For a moment she got tangled up in her own explanation, then her wariness returned. "He's a metal sculptor. He lives in the building straight across."

"The whole building?"

She looked at him for several seconds. "Listen. Thank you for your concern about me." She raised the beeper. "But I've got to check in."

"Yeah, I know. And I should get back to work." He stared into her green eyes and realized he didn't want to leave. "If you get into trouble, call me." He opened the door.

"Right," she said and made an attempt to smile.

THE NEWSPAPER wanted her to spend the next day at the county courthouse with a writer waiting for the verdict on a murder trial. The irony of the assignment wasn't lost on T.J. She'd been waiting for another verdict for two and a half years. Now she would have to photograph a different killer and a different family that had been torn apart by violence.

She would do her job as she'd been doing since her discovery, but she also needed to make some plans. And after being shot at, she knew she needed a better way to protect herself.

She hadn't mentioned her involvement in the drive-by shooting to her boss at the paper. The media had picked it up, however, and she'd had to refuse an interview for the six o'clock news. It was bad enough having to file a police report and give her name and address.

T.J. closed and locked the door to her darkroom, pushed aside the metal cabinet that held her photographic paper and pulled out the briefcase. She'd had to break the latch when she'd found it in her father's office, now it was held closed by several strips of gray duct tape. She pulled the tape free and opened the lid.

Nick DeSalvo seemed to think someone was after her. Or, maybe he only intended to scare her and see what she'd tell him. She couldn't tell him or anyone else the truth until she knew who to trust. She certainly couldn't trust Nick DeSalvo.

The gun rested on top of several file folders next to a rubber-banded stack of four audiotapes. It wasn't the gun that had killed her brother, but it had been used by a policeman to kill. The files and the tapes confirmed that fact. She carefully set the weapon on the counter then closed the lid and retaped the case.

A WOMAN OPENED the door to Jackson's building. Dressed in a leather miniskirt and a lace camisole, she looked as though she'd been magically transported from the streets of New York City to the west side of Atlanta. The classic beauty of her face was offset by dark, elaborately layered eye makeup and haphazardly dyed hair in a bright lipstick red.

The last time T.J. had seen this particular friend of Jackson's, her hair had been purple and she'd had even more skin exposed. "Hi, Rita. Is Jackson here?" T.J. held the briefcase clutched tightly to her chest.

"Hi . . ."

"T.J.," she supplied her name since it seemed to have slipped Rita's mind.

Rita's gaze rested on the briefcase for a moment before she answered. "He's in the back. You know the way?" She waited for T.J.'s nod of assent before she shrugged and raised a hand toward Jackson's living quarters. "I'm watching Oprah."

"Thanks," T.J. answered, glad that Rita wasn't the nosy type. She wanted to talk to Jackson alone.

A steel door decorated with an intricate series of welds that looked like a spiderweb separated Jackson's home from his studio. T.J. entered the unheated portion of the building and saw Jackson bending over an open fifty-gallon drum filled with something that looked like motor oil. One of the men who occasionally worked with him stood on the opposite side and between them they held a section of metalwork suspended by a long pipe.

T.J. waited as they dipped the metal into the liquid then moved it to hang in the air to dry.

"Bring up that other section and get it rigged," Jackson said to his helper, then wiped his hands on an orange rag as he turned to her. "Hey, T.J."

"Could I talk to you a minute—" her eyes drifted to the man working a short distance away "—alone?"

Jackson didn't hesitate. He stuffed the rag in the back pocket of his fatigue pants. "Gerry," he called. "Forget that for now. Why don't you go get us something to eat." He reached in his pocket and pulled out a few bills. "Take the van. And, ask Rita if she wants a pizza or somethin'."

Gerry took the money and left.

Jackson walked over to a circle of metal folding chairs and waited for her to follow. They both sat down. "What's so secret?" His eyes lowered to the briefcase for a moment. "You're holding that case like a terrorist with a bomb."

T.J. loosened her grip on the briefcase and settled it on her knees. She concentrated on being as honest as she could without getting Jackson in the middle of her problems. "I need a safe place to hide this for a while. And I can't tell you why."

The frown on Jackson's face nearly made T.J. lose her nerve. He looked ready to spring out of the chair. "Tell me it's not drugs or drug money." His voice carried the implacable sound of refusal. "You know when I was young and stupid I managed to get myself into some bad situations. It made my old man crazy because he couldn't stop me from screwing up my life. But I think your father and mine would probably march back from the other side if I helped *you* do something illegal."

"No— It's not . . . anything like that. It's a secret." Jackson's accusation made her stumble on her planned speech. "It's important, but not illegal." Heaven forbid he should take it to the police to protect her. Then they would come after him. "I swear." T.J. caught herself raising one hand like a Girl Scout and felt ridiculous. The very real danger might make her feel like a ten-year-old, but she wasn't going to act like one. She looked him in the eye. "And Jackson, if anything happens to me, I want you to burn it."

5

NICK HAD THE FEELING that something was wrong. Something besides the fact that he couldn't get T. J. Amberly out of his head. Her face haunted his thoughts like an intriguing unsolved mystery—along with the face in the photograph she'd taken. He currently had zip in the way of leads to find the driver of the car, and even less in figuring out T.J.

No matter how many times she denied it, Nick could tell she was afraid. He intended to find out why.

He'd called her seven times and had gotten her machine over and over. With each repetition of her recorded message his worry increased. Finally, a little before one in the afternoon, the thin thread of his patience had snapped and he'd called the paper.

It always amazed him how much information an authoritative voice could coerce from most citizens. The well-meaning assistant in the newspaper photo department had looked up the schedule and found T.J.'s name—assigned to the Andrew Whitman verdict.

The fact that Nick could easily find out T.J.'s schedule concerned him. Who else might do the same? The photo assistant had never even asked him to identify himself.

Instead of a leisurely lunch, Nick made his way downtown, to the county courthouse—one of the last places in the state that he wanted to be. And T.J. wouldn't want him there. He told himself that all he would do is find her, make sure she was okay. Then, he'd go back to his office.

He found her outside the courtroom in a hallway crowded with reporters and photographers. He remembered stepping out of a hearing and having to face the lights from the video cameras and the questions aimed like punches. He hadn't been able to answer their questions—not without revealing the lie. So most of the footage used on the news consisted of him pushing through the crowd with his lawyer stumbling after him.

As he took in the scene before him now, he wondered about the kind of person it took to dig through the dirt of someone's life just for the sake of a story. He didn't like the thought of lumping T.J. into that group, although he'd already witnessed her determination. Could she be as relentless as some of the reporters who'd come at him? He instantly pushed that thought away. He didn't want to delegate her to the opposing team. He wanted her on his side.

The media arrayed in the hallway seemed innocent enough. Most of them looked bored and passed the time reading or jotting down notes. Some of them joked with their competition. But T.J. was talking to a policeman. Officer Keith Nesmith—one of the men he'd been investigating.

That old warning instinct left over from his days on the force prickled up Nick's spine. Coincidence wasn't an option. And Nesmith was too controlled and too cold to be led by his zipper. If he'd singled out T.J. for a conversation, then he'd had a reason other than the fact that she was a good-looking female. Nick wanted to know that reason.

T.J.'s heart seemed to pause when she looked toward the far end of the hallway and into the probing stare of Nick DeSalvo. She felt a jolt of…relief. Some part of her was glad to see him. Glad for an excuse to get away from the man she'd been talking to. As DeSalvo made his way toward her and she recovered from her shock, the suspicions returned. What was he doing here?

The man who had engaged her in conversation noticed her drifting attention and turned to look in the same direction. His entire demeanor changed when he saw DeSalvo walking toward them.

He turned back to face her, looking grim. "Nice talking to you," he said to T.J. before moving away. He nodded to Nick as he passed him but didn't speak.

"What did he want?" Nick said without preamble. His intense gaze tracked the other man's progress down the hall as if at any moment he might spin around with a weapon.

"Are you following me?" T.J. asked fending off his dictatorial question. She couldn't let him know she'd been glad to see him, no matter how briefly. Besides, the feeling had passed. Now she was mad.

Nick shifted his unsmiling scrutiny to her. "What did he want?"

T.J. nervously glanced in the direction of the people closest to them to see if they were paying attention. DeSalvo was acting like a jealous husband and she barely knew the man. Well, that wasn't completely true. She knew some things about him—more than she wanted to know. Unfortunately, each time he got close, the first things she reacted to centered around the weight of his body on hers, the firm strength of his hands, the musky smell of his skin. Not the fact that he'd killed her brother and might very well hurt her, too.

Disgusted by her momentary weakness, she brought her attention back to the confrontation at hand and drew in a calming breath. She certainly didn't want to argue with him in the courthouse, to make a telling scene in front of all those people. Someone might remember him, or have been part of the coverage of her brother's death.

"Why do you want to know?"

Nick watched her as if he could will her to tell him. Then he crossed his arms like an inquisitor. "Because you seem to have a thing for police officers."

"What?" T.J. could hardly get the word out. The pounding of her heart had tightened her throat. "He's a—"

"—cop," Nick finished for her. "He didn't mention that to you?"

"No, he just started talking to me.... He wasn't in uniform. I—"

At that moment the doors to the courtroom were opened by an officer of the court and several people rushed out. Lights came on. Reporters grabbed their tape recorders or microphones. T.J. automatically reached for her camera and tested the flash.

"I have to shoot this," she said and moved into the crowd. Away from Nick DeSalvo. Away from her escalating fears. Away from the tendency to move closer to him. Somehow the police knew. DeSalvo was right. The shots must have been meant for her. As the group of reporters and photographers waited for the family of the victim, T.J. glanced in Nick's direction one more time. Ever since that day on the street, he'd been around her. Now he'd blatantly followed her downtown. Maybe he had arranged everything—the car, the shots . . . But if he did, why did he keep stepping between her and harm's way?

"How does it feel to finally get a guilty verdict?" one of the reporters asked the mother of the victim.

"I'm just glad that it's over." The woman's voice shook. "We can't bring our son back, but at least now we can go on with our lives."

T.J. pushed the shutter button and shot a few frames of the woman dabbing her eyes with a handkerchief. *Go on with our lives* . . . Her own eyes started filling and she angrily blinked the moisture away. The only way T.J. could go on was to risk her life. To tell the world about why her brother had died. She had to find the courage to see this through.

"We feel that the verdict has brought justice and some closure to this family in their time of grief," the lawyer cut in. He took the mother's arm and steered her toward the elevator. "Thank you all for coming."

Justice and closure. T.J. shot a few more frames of the group leaving while she searched for her own strength. Ready or not, she had to face what she'd begun. When she'd gone to the Save the Planet demonstration looking for Gina Tarantino, she thought she'd be safe in the crowd, that she could remain anonymous until she was ready. Until she had a plan of how to turn the evidence over to the...police. The good guys. But instead, she'd run directly into Nick DeSalvo and unwittingly set something in motion. Now, T.J. felt surrounded and outnumbered. She had to find someone to trust, someone to help. If she just had one person to depend on . . .

She turned and her gaze met Nick DeSalvo's. He stood next to her camera bag, waiting for her. He seemed solid . . . dependable. The urge to ask for help was so strong that for a moment she thought of walking over and blurting out the truth. Getting it all out in the open. As if he would want that.

Wrong. Nick wouldn't want to tell the world that his buddies had committed crimes, that one of them had left the evidence then killed himself. Nick would want to keep it a secret, to hide it away, to shut her up. Like he had silenced her father by killing her brother.

She knew she had to keep her distance, and to keep him away from her before she did something stupid, like trust him.

As she moved in his direction, Nick decided that if T. J. Amberly were his woman, he'd try to talk her into another line of work. She looked as if she needed a stiff drink, or a strong shoulder to lean on. Why did women like her think they had to do everything on their own?

"Do you always get so emotionally involved with your work?" he asked as she approached him.

"What do you mean?" T.J. made a great show of stowing her camera equipment, avoiding his eyes.

"You looked like you were about to cry."

She glanced up at him. Beyond sad or angry, she seemed hurt.

"Don't you think it's sad? Don't you feel bad for that family? They lost their son . . ."

Nick ran a hand down his face trying to get his own emotions under control. He remembered a boy who'd died. But, this wasn't his hearing, the end of his career—all of that had been decided two and a half years ago. He didn't need to take his anger and frustration with his own choices out on T. J. Amberly. "At least the law gave them some justice," he said, unable and unwilling to delve any deeper. "Someone got dead, someone went to prison. That's the way it's supposed to work."

"Really?" She watched him and the look in her eyes made him uneasy.

"I used to be a cop," he added in justification.

She didn't look surprised. She rose to her feet and swung the heavy camera bag onto her shoulder. "Well then, you should understand perfectly what I'm about to tell you. If you keep following me, I'll have you arrested for harassment." She turned to leave.

"Wait a minute—" Without weighing the consequences, he grabbed her arm. "I need to know why Nesmith wanted to talk to you. It's important."

She didn't answer. She simply looked at his hand on her arm, then back up at him. The warning was clear.

He let go and she walked away.

T.J. STARED AT her own reflection overlapping that of the blinking lights on the Christmas tree in the window of Victoria's Secret. She couldn't believe she'd actually gone Christmas shopping. Was she losing her mind?

She'd had to do something. After leaving the courthouse she'd gone to the paper, dropped off the film and written out captions for the photos. Then, instead of going home, she'd driven to the mall. An attempt to act normal, to pretend that she had a life, family and friends.

She bought a classic art nouveau candleholder for Tyler, the manager of the Coach Works, and cards to send to her friends from school. She hadn't been able to decide about the proper gift for Jackson, so she'd left that dilemma for another day. As she stared unseeingly into the reflections, her mind was on the one purchase that made the others seem surreal. She'd stopped at a gun shop near the mall and bought bullets for what she now knew was a nine millimeter automatic.

She'd taken the gun out of the case before she'd visited Jackson. Now, if she had to use it to protect herself, she had bullets to do it.

T.J. sighed and focused on the beautiful lingerie accented by Christmas ribbon and ornaments displayed in the window before her. She wished her life could be normal, that she could smile, walk into the store and buy something beautiful to wear for her lover. Nick DeSalvo's image flared in her mind and she angrily pushed the fantasy away. He wasn't her lover, he was her target. No matter how instantaneously her body reacted to his.

And she could never be normal again.

Until three years ago, her life had been so simple. Even though her mother had died when T.J. was ten, T.J.'s father had always been there for her. He'd done his best with her and her brother, Rusty. Sure, they'd had some problems, Rusty in particular. He'd run with the wrong crowd, experimented with some drugs. But, they were a family.

Even after Rusty's death, she'd been able to cling to the dream of having her own family. But then her father died and she'd discovered the briefcase. Grief for Rusty's unavenged murder and fear for her own safety if she pursued the issue had blacked out her dreams.

Now she couldn't see anything bright or happy in the future. Not even Christmas.

T.J. hiked her packages a little higher, gave the fragile white lace gown in the window a wistful look then headed for the exit. It was time to go home.

She had her keys in her hand and her eyes focused on her car in the parking lot when something hit her from behind. The impact made her drop the packages in an effort to brace herself. As she went down, she felt her purse being yanked away.

"Hey!" she yelled as she hit the pavement.

The man never even slowed down as he ran past her.

T.J. pushed to her feet and watched him sprint through the parking lot toward the main road and four lanes of traffic.

"Damn!" She was more angry than afraid. Why hadn't she taken karate in college when she'd had the opportunity? Although, the whole thing had happened so fast, she wouldn't have had a chance to use any of it. Nick hadn't been there to save her this time.

"Damn," she muttered again and bent to pick up her packages. She noticed that her elbow was bleeding but it didn't hurt yet. As she walked back to the mall to report the purse snatching, she tried to remember what she'd had in her purse.

Not much cash, maybe twenty bucks or so. But all her credit cards and her identification would have to be replaced. "Damn."

THE FLAMES OF of the candles in the center of T.J.'s dining table danced as the furnace kicked on. She sat with a pad in front of her and a pen in her hand. She'd been writing a list of allies and enemies, safety and danger. Unfortunately, Nick DeSalvo's name came up on both sides of the sheet.

She rubbed a palm against her forehead, then took another sip of wine. She wished she could talk to her father, just one last time.

Tears came to her eyes. If she could talk to her dad or Rusty she'd want to spend the time telling them she loved them and missed them, not asking for help. But she needed help. Now, in the land of the living.

She sniffed back the tears. Jackson would help her. His name was at the top of the list. But he wasn't home tonight. That left her alone, again.

T.J. pushed the pad away, picked up her glass of wine and headed for the stairs. In the loft, she stopped to pull on a jacket before swinging open the trapdoor to the roof.

The night was clear and cool. The skyline of the city was sparkling, yet remote. T.J. turned her back on it. No help there. She sat on the edge of the balcony and faced the parking lot and warehouses situated across the street. She'd wait for Jackson to come home, then she'd tell him everything. About the car and the shots . . . and her brother. She'd explain that piece by piece her life was under attack.

Today, someone had stolen her purse, her identity. It could have been a coincidence. But T.J. couldn't afford to ignore anything. Who knew what might happen tomorrow?

She absently scanned the cars in the lot illuminated by circles of light, looking for Jackson's van.

That's when she saw the movement. A man, leaning against a car in the darker part of the lot. T.J. squinted to see him better but the darkness hid his features. Was he waiting for someone to come out?

Or for someone to come in . . .

T.J. thought of Jackson and felt uneasy. What if the man in the dark was a mugger? Her recent experience ached like a fresh wound. What if a criminal was waiting for one of the unsuspecting residents of the Coach Works to park and walk to the building? The lot was posted as private property. If he didn't live here, he shouldn't be there. T.J. slowly pushed up and headed for the phone to dial 911.

The operator asked her name, her loft number, and then told her to stay on the line and watch the suspicious person until the police arrived.

It took them eight minutes. As the patrol car rolled through the gate, the officer inside switched on a spotlight. The light illuminated the man and T.J. thought her vision had begun playing tricks. She hung up the phone, raced downstairs, and headed for the parking lot.

It was Nick DeSalvo.

By the time T.J. reached him, the officers had him facing the car with his hands on the hood. One of them held what T.J. assumed was Nick's gun. An-

other police car pulled into the lot as one of the officers turned to T.J.

"Did you call about a suspicious person, ma'am?"

DeSalvo turned his head and looked at her. Staring into his dark eyes, her voice failed her. She nodded, but the "yes" came out as more of a croak.
Everyone seemed to be waiting for her to do something. T.J. cleared her throat and approached De-
Salvo.

"What are you doing here?" she asked.

His eyes shifted to the two officers getting out of the
second car. His whole body seemed to tighten. "I was
in the neighborhood, and thought I'd say hello." He
wasn't looking at her as he spoke. The answer
sounded distracted, automatic.

"I told you not to follow me anymore."

Before he could reply another voice cut through the
pause.

"Has this man been bothering you, ma'am?"

T.J. watched as one of the newly arrived policemen strolled forward. Instead of being relieved by his
concern, T.J. felt an unreasonable surge of alarm. The
solution suddenly seemed disproportionate to the
problem. The second officer riding along was the man
she'd spoken to at the courthouse . . . Nesmith. A
feeling of dread and something like betrayal made her
wish she could call the whole thing off. She didn't
want to discuss her concerns about Nick DeSalvo with
these men.

"Uh . . . Well, he . . ."

"What's your problem, DeSalvo?" The officer went on, without waiting for her answer.

"No problem, lieutenant." Nick's mouth slanted with a bitter smile. Just what he needed after a long day, another round with Lieutenant Echols. "Long time, no see."

The lieutenant's face went hard. "Put your right hand behind your back," he ordered.

Nick took a moment to consider his options, then complied. He'd be better off at the station, around a lot of witnesses, than in a dark parking lot resisting arrest. The lieutenant grabbed Nick's hand and snapped a handcuff around his wrist. He jerked Nick's other arm backward and completed cuffing him. Then he put one hand in the middle of Nick's back and shoved him forward until his cheekbone struck the hood of the car.

"W-wait! What are you doing?" T.J. sputtered. Nick could hear the genuine alarm in her voice and it took some of the pain out of his abrupt meeting with the hood of the cruiser.

The lieutenant ignored her. "I told you when you were on the force not to screw around with me," he growled close to Nick's ear. "Now that you're a civilian, your ass is *mine*."

"What am I being charged with?" Nick asked, controlling his urge to tell Echols where he could shove his threats.

"Whatever I decide on," Echols replied and pulled Nick upright.

T.J. grabbed the lieutenant's arm. "I said, wait a second!"

Nesmith yanked her away.

"Let her go," Nick demanded. Nesmith had finally managed to tick him off. Seeing his hand on T.J.'s arm set off some primal alarm in Nick. He pulled away from the lieutenant and faced the other cop.

Just then, headlights flashed across the group and a van stopped behind one of the police cars. The lieutenant took out his nightstick and stepped within swinging distance of Nick to his right.

"Jackson!" T.J. called out as she recognized the driver.

Jackson approached the policemen with a man and a woman following. "What the hell is going on here?" His unfriendly gaze fell on Officer Nesmith, the man holding T.J.'s arm.

Good, Nick thought, the more the merrier. The odds seemed to be shifting. The first two officers who'd arrived on the scene moved over to intercept this new group. "This is police business, stay back."

Jackson kept moving. "That woman is my business," Jackson said, indicating T.J. "I'm not leaving until I talk to her."

Nick twisted in Jackson's direction. "Get her out of here," he ordered, oblivious to his own predicament.

Nesmith released T.J.'s arm. With one scathing look in the officer's direction, she headed for Jackson. Lieutenant Echols prodded Nick in the lower back with his nightstick and yanked him toward the patrol car. He walked on his own. As long as T.J. wasn't in-cluded, he'd play Echols's game.

He wished Jackson would hurry up and get her the hell out of here, but everyone remained stubbornly present. He met her worried gaze right before Echols shoved him into the back seat of the cruiser. Then he watched her turn to Jackson and something twisted inside him. He wanted her to turn to him.

After what must have been a hurried explanation of events, Jackson walked toward the car.

"What are you arresting him for?" he asked the lieutenant.

Lieutenant Echols looked satisfied with the out-come of the evening. "Well, let's see. I guess it would be trespassing on private property."

"Who's pressing charges?"

Echols pinned T.J. with his gaze. She crossed her arms and shook her head. "He didn't do anything. I saw a man in the parking lot and called the police. I didn't know it was DeSalvo. I don't want him to go to jail over this."

"If DeSalvo doesn't live here, then the owner will press charges, as soon as I call him. This lot is posted private property," Echols said and signaled for Nes-mith to get in the car.

Jackson's mouth angled into a smirk and Nick held his breath. They might all end up in jail tonight.

"The owner's a personal friend of mine, and so is this guy. I think there's been a mistake. This friend of mine—" he indicated Nick "—was just waiting for me to come home. If you arrest anybody, you should arrest me for being late." When no one moved or answered, he added, "If you think a crime has been committed, maybe you should just take us both, then my lawyer can make one trip." The threat was clear.

Echols looked skeptical but glanced at the first two officers who had arrived on the scene. "Who called this in?"

One of the officer's pointed to T.J. "She did."

If looks were bullets... Nick thought as he watched the lieutenant's eyes go hard. *Let it go, T.J., don't give him a reason to remember you.*

"Do you know the penalty for making a false report? I could arrest you right now...."

T.J. stood firm in the face of his anger but she looked shaken. Nick watched in admiration as she drew herself up straighter. "I'm sorry. Like Jackson said, it was a mistake," she informed him stiffly.

"Get him out of my car," Echols barked at Nesmith before sliding behind the wheel.

A moment later, Nick stood with Jackson and T.J. watching the police cars roll out of the parking lot. She'd warned him to stay away from her and she'd made good on her threat to have him *nearly* arrested. Defending his position in her life was hard, but considering the incidents over the last few days, he knew he had to be here—for T.J. Somebody had to look out for her and since he was the one losing sleep over her safety, he intended to give her his complete attention. And now Echols was involved.

Nick replaced his gun and wallet. "Thanks, but you shouldn't get between the lieutenant and his problem with me," he said to Jackson.

Jackson gave him a cold look. "I didn't do it for you." He turned to T.J. "Let's get inside."

Nick was about to be shut out. He couldn't allow that to happen. He knew Jackson was protecting her, but Jackson didn't understand the danger. "I need to talk to you," Nick said to T.J.

T.J. seemed undecided.

"Now." When she looked mutinous, he added, "Please."

"Come inside," T.J. answered finally.

"Let's go," Jackson said and tugged T.J. toward Rita and Gerry. When the group entered the inner door, Jackson faced Nick. "I'm only going to say this once. If you do anything to hurt her, you'd better be looking over your shoulder, 'cause I'll be there. And you won't like me when I'm mad."

"I don't particularly like you now," Nick responded, remembering the way he'd felt when T.J. had looked to Jackson for help. "But if you're a friend of *Ms.* Amberly's then at least we're on the same side."

Jackson turned to T.J. "I need to know what's going on . . . and soon," he said.

"I know. I'll come over tomorrow. I promise. And Jackson . . ."

He hesitated, looking uncomfortable. "Yeah?"

"Thanks."

Jackson's gaze met Nick's for a millisecond, in triumph or warning, before connecting with T.J.'s again. "Anytime," he said, then pushed the door release and ushered Rita through it. T.J., Nick and Gerry followed.

Nick walked with T.J. to her loft and waited as she opened the unlocked door and stepped inside. "Why do you always call me *Ms.* in that disapproving tone of—"

As soon as the door closed, Nick's hands clamped on her upper arms. He spun her around and pushed her against the wall. Apparently too shocked to fight, T.J. gazed up at him as his mouth came down on hers. The kiss was hard and angry and worried, giving away more of the emotional turmoil inside him than he wanted to show.

He pulled back as suddenly as he'd pressed forward. Then, he rested his jaw close to her ear and sighed. "I think I'm losing my mind." He loosened the tense grip on her arms, sliding his hands upward.

He looked into T.J.'s green eyes and saw her surprise, her confusion. She hadn't recovered enough to be angry. He couldn't let her go just yet. "Might as well commit the crime if I'm gonna pay the price," he said as his fingers framed her face and slid into her hair. He didn't want to give her the chance to think, to push him away before he . . . He lowered his mouth to hers once more, gently, coaxingly and hoped like hell she wouldn't punch him.

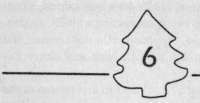

6

SHE DIDN'T PUNCH HIM. Nick felt a quiver run through T.J., as if she'd been asleep and he'd surprised her awake. The sweetness of it made him hard. He kissed her thoroughly, tasting the tang of wine, the smooth glide of her tongue. Then he felt her hands shift and push against his chest.

She dragged her mouth free. "Stop . . . please."

He didn't move for a few seconds. The touch of her hands and the nearness of her mouth was too tempting.

Her hands pushed harder. "I don't want—"

He backed away.

T.J. smoothed her fingers over her clothes as if she needed them as protection. But she wouldn't look at him. He slid his hands into his back pockets so that he wouldn't be tempted again. "I'm sorry."

She stepped around him and moved toward the kitchen. If she'd shouted or slapped him he would have felt better. Instead, she approached the sink, filled a teakettle and set it on a burner of the stove.

Nick ran a hand over his face. He could still taste her and his body seemed to be holding that thought. He tried to regain his control. "I'm sorry. I shouldn't have done that."

"You're right, you shouldn't have," she said, still avoiding his gaze.

"Look, I—"

"No, you look." She turned toward him, crossing her arms and rubbing the places where his hands had been. "I don't know what you want from me, but we're not friends, we're not doing business and we're not . . . dating. I meant it when I said I'd have you arrested if you didn't stop following me."

Nick didn't like the course of the conversation, but he couldn't stand there and let the obvious go by. "Then why didn't you let them take me in?"

Why hadn't she? T.J. turned away from him again, opened a cabinet and took down two cups. She had to keep busy, to ignore the fact that she'd just been thoroughly kissed by the man she was sworn to destroy . . . and enjoyed it. Her body had turned traitor. His mouth . . . He tasted like Spearmint gum and he'd kissed her like a starving man, like he needed her to breathe. And she'd responded to that need, to his warm lips and his urgency.

"I changed my mind. I didn't like their attitude."

"Their attitude?"

She kept the conversation on a safe path—away from acknowledging her own racing pulse and the craziness of wanting to be kissed again. "Why did they treat you that way? I thought cops took care of their own."

"Echols and I have some history. It's another long story."

"Sit down and tell me so I don't feel like a fool for bringing you in instead of waving you off to jail."

"Believe me, from what I've seen of you I can say one thing. You're no fool."

Oh, yes I am, she thought to herself. The fact that Nick DeSalvo was standing in her loft talking to her proved it. She studied him silently and tried to find her anger, the determination to tell him to get out of her life. But all she could think about was the warmth of his mouth and the insistent touch of his hands. "Coffee, or tea?" she managed to say.

"Isn't there supposed to be an 'or me?' in there?"

T.J. rolled her eyes. "Which would you like?"

"I'd like you."

The playful, alluring sound of his voice brought the conversation to a conspicuous halt. T.J.'s mind went completely blank as warmth moved up her neck.

He shrugged and smiled, then let her off the hook. "Whatever you're having."

A few moments later, the two of them were sitting on the leather sofa in the living area, each holding a cup of tea.

T.J. held her cup in a death grip and searched for a safe topic. One that didn't include liking or wanting. She wanted to talk about justice. "Does this problem with the lieutenant have something to do with your being fired?"

Nick's teasing gaze turned hard.

"How do you know about that?"

Sticking to the technical truth seemed the safest course. "I uh, I checked you out through the newspaper," she admitted.

He looked away. "No. It wasn't because of the inquiry. When I was on the force . . ." He put his cup down and stood up. He walked to the front window and looked out into the dark courtyard. "A buddy of mine was involved with something . . . something illegal, I think. Anyway, Lieutenant Echols is part of it. Or, he knows about it. And I've been trying to find out the truth."

T.J. knew the truth—she had evidence. She decided to test DeSalvo's acting ability. "Why don't you ask your friend?"

Nick pivoted to look at her. "Because he's dead. He killed himself on Christmas Eve three years ago."

There it was again, the bitterness. He didn't seem hurt, he seemed angry. T.J. knew that kind of anger; it was the kind that kept you focused on why something happened rather than giving in to the grief. He might have been a dirty cop, but he'd cared about his friend. "Tell me about it."

"What's to tell?" Nick shrugged. "He left a note saying he was sorry, then he ate his gun."

"Ate his gun?"

"Put his gun in his mouth and blew his brains out."

T.J. thought of the loss she'd felt at Rusty's death, the unanswered questions . . . the anger. Nick should be nominated for an academy award for his convincing performance. How could he appear angry and confused about his friend when he knew they'd all been guilty. "That must have been terrible for his family," she said, contributing to the performance.

Nick drew in a slow breath and released it. "Yeah, it was." He looked past her for a moment, staring at nothing. "You remember Gina Tarantino? The female officer you photographed?"

T.J. nodded.

"She was his wife."

A slight twinge of conscience pricked T.J. So they'd all suffered. It didn't seem possible that Nick and Gina could have killed Rusty after knowing how much the loss of a loved one hurt. Yet T.J. knew the truth, didn't she?

Nick moved back across the room, but instead of sitting down, he changed the subject. "Now I want to know why Lieutenant Echols and Nesmith are so interested in you."

"What do you mean?"

"This area of town isn't their beat. Either they picked up my name on the radio or they're watching you."

"Why would they be watching me?"

"You tell me."

"I don't know. Maybe because I've been involved in a lot of things lately—the demonstration, the shooting, being mugged."

"Mugged?"

"Some guy snatched my purse today at the mall."

"Did he hurt you?"

T.J.'s hand automatically moved to her skinned elbow but she refused to whine. "No. He just got a little money, all my credit cards and ID."

Nick's gaze was on her arm. "Let me see." Nick pulled T.J. to her feet.

"It's nothing," T.J. protested but Nick continued to push up her sleeve. His hands were warm on her skin and his touch was light. The dark expression on his face made her nervous.

"Did you report it?"

"Yes, at the mall. But they'll never catch him. I didn't even see him that well myself. He hit me from behind."

Nick pulled her sleeve back down but he looked worried. That made T.J. even more nervous.

"Something is going on. I can't help if you don't tell me the truth."

After days of questioning everything, suddenly T.J. wasn't sure she was ready to hear the truth. "What do you mean?"

"There have been too many incidents in a row to be coincidence. I know you're afraid of something. Are you sure some old boyfriend isn't stalking you?"

He'd asked the question, but to T.J. he didn't look serious about the answer. And she wouldn't justify it with a reply. Even if he was still holding her arm.

"Why are you so interested in my old boyfriends?"

"I'm worried about you," he said. His fingers moved over her forearm and a tingle of pleasure moved under her skin, upward and outward.

She pulled her arm away. "Thank you, but . . ."

The intercom buzzed. Happy for the interruption, T.J. crossed to the speaker and pushed the button to answer.

"T.J.? I need to see you at the outer door," David, the night security man said.

"Ask him why," Nick prompted.

"Why?" T.J. asked.

"There's something strange out here with your name on it. I thought you should look at it before I call the police."

"I'll be right there."

Nick didn't give her the opportunity to argue about whether or not he was going with her. "Let's go," he said and opened the door.

As they stepped out of the outer door into the cold, the security man pointed up. There, hanging from a nail about seven feet from ground level was a purse with a piece of paper taped to it. The paper had T. J. Amberly written in bold black letters.

"That's my purse," T.J. said.

David produced a broom and proceeded to lift the purse down.

T.J. bent to pick it up, but Nick stopped her.

"Let me do it."

Visions of old Halloween pranks ran through her mind, along with the very real fear that now, who-ever stole her purse had come to where she lived.

David moved closer and shone his flashlight on the bag. Nick squatted down and gingerly opened the clasp. He pulled the bag open with two fingers and the security man illuminated the contents. Everything looked normal. Nick flipped the bag upside down and dumped the contents on the sidewalk.

"See anything strange?" Nick asked.

Beyond being embarrassed by the junk she normally carried around in her purse, T.J. knelt down next to Nick and examined the contents. A brush and two lipsticks, a beat-up pack of gum. Tissues and cash register receipts, her business planner and her wallet.

Nick picked up her wallet and opened the snap. T.J. was amazed. Everything was there. Eighteen dollars and change, all her credit cards, her driver's license... everything. She looked up at Nick and felt a true shudder of fear. The thief hadn't taken anything.... Then why...

Nick started stuffing the contents back in the bag and T.J. helped. He stood, handed the bag to T.J. and turned to the security guard.

"Did you see who left this?"

"No. We were on shift change. When I came out to do a door check, I found it. Should I call the police and make a report?"

"No." Nick answered so fast that T.J. didn't have a chance to reply. "Thanks, I'll take care of it."

The man looked at T.J. "Are you sure?" he asked.

"Yeah, it's okay, David. I guess someone is just playing a practical joke on me. Thanks for finding it."

Back in her loft, T.J. dropped her bag on the counter and turned to face Nick DeSalvo. The time for tact was over.

"You want to tell me what kind of game you're playing here?"

"Me? What the hell are you talking about?"

"You don't think it's a little odd that from the very first moment you literally ran into me, my life has become a veritable crime wave?"

"Why do you think it's *my* fault?"

T.J. walked away from him. "I don't know what to think except that I need to stay away from you."

"Have you noticed that I seem to be the only one who gives a damn about what's happening to you?"

"Jackson—"

"Jackson?" Nick repeated disparagingly. "You're dealing with the big leagues now." His expression changed as a new thought occurred to him. "Is he your lover, is that what you're trying to say?"

"No," T.J. answered before she thought. She wished she'd lied. Maybe that would get Nick to back off. "He's a friend, though it's none of your business."

"I'm making it my business. I care about you. I'm here, and I can help you. It's time to start telling the truth."

He reached out and drew her forward. "You know I didn't steal your purse . . . or shoot at you. I was standing next to you at the time." He slowly enveloped her in his arms, ignoring the fact that she remained stiff as a statue. He spoke into her hair, low and coaxingly. "Tell me why you're afraid. We may not be friends, or in business, or dating, but we're sure as hell not strangers anymore. And I can't ignore what's going on."

He ran his hands up her back and the stiffness disappeared. She leaned into him and pressed her face into his shoulder.

"I don't trust the police," she said, matching his low tone. He had to strain to hear the words. "And I don't trust you."

"Me?" He sounded amused. "I'm the safest guy you know."

"No, you're not," she added, then stopped to take a deep breath.

Nick could feel every contour of her body. With each breath, her breasts rose and fell, teasing his chest with their softness. He wanted to undress her, slowly, and touch those breasts. Make love to them with his mouth, his tongue. But first he had to get the truth out of her.

"Why don't you trust the police? What have you done?"

T.J. floated in the comfort of his embrace and tried to put a successful lie together. She'd told the truth so far but now she had to settle on a story. Hopefully one he would believe. *The safest guy you know*... Now that was a lie if she'd ever heard one. And standing in his arms and wishing it was true would only get her into more serious trouble.

"I got a tip," she mumbled into his shirt.

"What?" He rearranged his arms and pulled her face closer to his.

"An anonymous phone call about some bad cops."

Nick's arms tightened and he pushed her away so he could look into her eyes. "When? And why would they call you?"

The look in his eyes was frightening. T.J. almost lost the skein of her lie. "Because I work for the paper. They wanted someone to investigate."

"When did you get the call?" he asked again.

T.J. remembered all the hang-ups she'd gotten after her picture of the criminal had been published on the front page. She needed to keep the lie as close to the truth as possible or she'd never pull it off. "Right after the demonstration. I got this call and the next thing I know, you're here and the police are here and . . ."

Nick ran a hand through his hair and just stared at her. "What did they tell you?"

"Not much. Just that some members of the county police needed to see the inside of a courtroom—from the defendant's point of view." He looked so alarmed that T.J.'s heart pounded even harder. She hadn't really expected him to believe the lie. She shrugged, trying to defuse the effect of her words. "I didn't really take it seriously—"

"Someone is taking *you* seriously."

"So, it's true?"

"Yeah, I believe it's true, and you sure as hell don't need to get involved."

"I don't want to." T.J. didn't need to lie about that. The fact that Nick would admit to her that there were some bad cops didn't make her feel any safer. Her life was under siege and the star suspect was staring at her. She wished she could forget the whole thing. But she couldn't forget her brother, Rusty.

"Who have you talked to about this?"

T.J. spoke the truth before she thought. "Just you."

He looked as if he were waiting for the rest of the story. When she didn't elaborate, he pushed.

"You must have said something or asked questions or...taken pictures." He leveled a fierce gaze at her. "Have you been taking pictures of cops?"

"A few, maybe...but—"

"I don't believe this! Who made you Wonder Woman? Don't you get it? You could get hurt."

"I didn't start getting hurt until I met you."

He ignored the jab. "Tell me who and where and when."

"How do I know you're not one of them?"

"If I am, you've already told me too much."

Nick watched T.J.'s expression change, saw the fear in her eyes and felt like swearing. She had more guts than good sense.

What delusion made her think she could take on men like Echols? Did she think being a member of the press made her invincible? These cops would fight back, and a cornered criminal hiding within the law was infinitely more dangerous than your basic felon.

Hell, he'd been nosing around for three years without finding any direct evidence against them. How could T.J. think that a few pictures would be enough?

"First of all I want you to promise me to take a vacation. It's almost Christmas. Why don't you go visit family, get out of town for a while?"

"I don't have any family," T.J. said in a tight, emotionless voice.

"None at all?"

"No," she answered firmly. End of discussion.

Rather than badger the truth out of her, Nick moved to the next best solution. "So, go see my family. They're up in Buffalo. That should be far enough. Take a coat, it's cold."

"I'm not going anywhere."

Nick didn't like the sound of that. He couldn't tell if she was stubborn or just plain nuts. "Why? Do you enjoy being harassed? Do you think you've got some big exclusive story that'll impress your friends and make your career?"

"Leaving town isn't an option. This is what I do. I work for the newspaper."

"Dammit, T.J. I'm trying to help here, but you're going to have to come up with something better than your job as a reason. We're talking about your life. These men aren't going to stand around with their arms crossed waiting for you to expose them."

"How do you know so much about it?"

"Because I used to be a cop. I know how they think, what they're capable of doing once they've stepped over the line."

"Did you tell them to watch me?"

Nick had to stop and take a deep breath. Why did she always come back to accusing him? "What did I ever do to make you think I'd hurt you?"

"Why were you fired from the police force?"

A series of fleeting images flashed through Nick's thoughts. A boy with a gun, Gina, the hospital. Then the investigation and the trial. He couldn't explain it away without exposing the lie, breaking his word. Some things were better left in the past.

"For doing my job," he answered, refusing to rise to the question-for-question bait.

"Your job is to shoot people?"

"Sometimes, yes."

He stared into her eyes. He thought of the demonstration, of the pictures T.J. had taken of him and Gina. "Have you been investigating me, too?"

7

"SHOULD I BE?"

Nick couldn't believe his ears. Or his eyes. T.J. was taking her paranoia a little too far. Facing him down as if he'd hurt her, as if he'd already committed some crime against her. "Ask me whatever you want to know."

"Were you one of the bad cops?"

He thought of just walking out, letting her fend for herself. If she didn't trust him, he couldn't change her mind. But the truth was all he had left of his career. "No."

"Then help me find out who they are and expose them."

Nick shook his head. "I'm not getting you involved. It's not worth it."

"It's worth it to me. If you're not involved, what do you have to lose?"

He'd already lost Mike. What else did he have to lose? He couldn't think of a damn thing except T. J. Amberly. "I thought you were trying to get rid of me. Now you suddenly want to be partners. Why?"

"Because what you said made sense. You know these men, I don't."

"Not good enough. Why?"

Because I want to believe you didn't murder Rusty,
T.J.'s mind whispered. Then she felt a stab of guilt.
She'd gone from being determined to prove Nick's
crime to hoping she was wrong. What was happening to her?

"Because you said you're the best one to help me.
I've decided to take you at your word."

He looked skeptical.

"Your word is good, isn't it?"

His skeptical gaze turned murderous. T.J. thought
she might have pushed him too far. But after several
heartbeats of silence, he answered.

"It's good. How's yours?"

"I'm working on it," T.J. said and forced a smile.

"That's comforting." Nick pulled a small address
book out of his back pocket. "I need to make some
calls."

"You can use that phone," T.J. said, indicating the
one on the kitchen counter.

While Nick made his calls, T.J. wandered around
the loft putting things back in place, rinsing out the
coffee cups, anything to stay out of Nick's line of sight.
His gaze followed her as he explained the events of the
evening to the people on the other end of the line. T.J.
still wasn't ready to face him when he hung up.

"Do you have an extra toothbrush in this place?"

"Why?"

Nick sauntered over and took a long measuring
look at the leather couch. "It's already midnight. I

thought I might play guard dog tonight to make sure you don't have any more unexpected excitement."

"There's no need for that. I have a security system and neighbors."

Nick planted his hands on his hips. "Tell me you didn't have an extra key in your purse, or a slip of paper with your security code written on it."

T.J.'s breath froze in her chest. She did keep an extra key in her purse, inside the zipper pocket. She moved over to see if the thief had found it.

Nick simply shook his head and stretched out on the couch to gauge the length. By the time she stood gazing down at him, he looked completely at home, legs crossed at the ankles and his hands braced behind his head.

"Did you find it?"

"Yes," she replied triumphantly. Nick didn't seem impressed.

"How long did the perp have your purse?"

T.J. couldn't see what difference that made but she thought about it. "Around half a day."

"How long does it take to have a duplicate key made?"

T.J. felt like socking him, just for being right. Her frown must have been answer enough.

"All right then, I'll stay on your couch tonight and tomorrow you can have the building manager change the locks."

T.J. wanted to argue but she was more afraid of the unknown harassers than she was of Nick DeSalvo.

Better the devil you know... Instinctively she knew that his offer was genuine. He'd protected her enough in the last few days. She didn't want to probe too deeply into his reasons for doing so, or her reasons for allowing it. Right now, she'd play along.

"The bathroom is down the hall," she said, giving in without making a big deal of it. "There's a toothbrush in the right-hand drawer near the sink. Towels in the cabinet."

"Why don't you have a Christmas tree?"

"What?" T.J. asked, trying to shift mental gears.

"Christmas is a few days away and you don't have a tree or any lights. What are you, some kind of Scrooge?"

T.J. glared at him. She didn't have a Christmas tree because she had nothing to celebrate and no one to celebrate with. Her only bright spot had been her objective to ruin Nick DeSalvo's new life. And recently, the anticipation of his downfall had lost some of its appeal.

"I just haven't gotten around to it," she lied. If she was lucky, she'd stay so busy that Christmas would come and go without her having to think about it too much. It would only make her sad.

Nick stared at her as if he could see right through her excuses, as if he'd ignored Christmas at some point in the past. T.J. looked away. She didn't want him to know anything else about her, and she didn't want to know about him. But most of all, she didn't want to give a damn if he ever celebrated Christmas again.

TOSSING IN HER OWN BED later that night, T.J. came to the conclusion that she was out of her league. She'd begun with a vendetta against one man and ended up antagonizing half the police force from the look of it. She sat up and pushed the hair out of her face. She had to depend on Nick. There was no one else.

What would her dad think about that? Or Rusty?

T.J. stood and walked to the stairs. Normally she might have gone down to the kitchen for a cup of hot chocolate or a glass of milk. But tonight, for the first time since she'd moved in, she wasn't alone in her loft. Nick DeSalvo was camped on her couch, her own personal bodyguard.

She sat down on the top step and looked out the front windows. The view, accented by the white, twinkling Christmas lights in the windows of Tyler's home across the yard was familiar but not very soothing. She needed someone to confide in, someone to help her off this limb she'd climbed out on. She knew her dad would want her to forget the whole thing and leave. He wouldn't want her hurt. Just as he'd sent her away to school to protect her after Rusty's death. But her heart needed to see this through. She was the last of her family. She had to find justice for her brother's death and for her father's years of worry.

Life might not be fair but she could help it along.

Just then a shadow moved across the windows. T.J.'s heart seemed to leap in her chest, and her hand gripped the bannister. Before she could do anything but breathe, the silhouette took on normal proportions and she recognized Nick. Obviously, he hadn't been able to sleep, either. In the dim light she could see that he'd removed his shirt along with his shoes and socks. The relaxed position of his body looked as though he were perfectly at ease in her home. Only the fact that he was awake in the middle of the night staring out of the windows betrayed his tension.

She studied the angle of his shoulder and the strong lines of his back, his tousled hair. An odd, wistfulness filled her. How many times had she dreamed of spending nights with someone she wanted...someone she loved. If he was any other man she could indulge her curiosity. She could walk down the stairs, move up behind him, put her arms around him and press herself to his back. Then he would turn and kiss her....

As if reading her thoughts, Nick turned. T.J.'s gaze moved over the width of bare chest shadowed by dark hair. A slow simmering heat warmed her thighs and belly. The glimmer of his eyes snared her. She had no idea how well he could see her in the dark, but she couldn't turn away.

He slowly walked to the foot of the stairs.

"Are you all right?" he asked.

Her voice came out in a strangled whisper. "Yes."

He propped one bare foot on the first step and T.J. felt a wave of fear. If he walked up the stairs she might just pull him into her arms, and lead him to her bed.

She made an effort to get her feet under her, then stood.

"I'm fine," she said in a stronger voice. "Couldn't sleep."

"Me, either." His voice was low, like a caress. His hand moved to the bannister. As T.J. watched his fingers curl around the polished wood she felt as though he were reaching for her instead. "Do you want to come down?"

"No," she whispered, fighting the coaxing tone of his voice.

"You sure? I don't bite."

With a stab of irritation bordering on jealousy she wondered how many other women had been mesmerized by the sexy promise in his voice. Her surprised reaction to that thought caused her to take a step backward.

"No. I mean . . . yes, I'm sure. I think I'm safer up here."

His wolfish smile flashed across the dark planes of his face. It had nothing to do with humor. "I could come up. . . ." He left the sentence hanging.

"You gave your word."

"I gave my word to protect you. Believe me, if you invite me up those stairs, nothing I do will hurt you."

You've already hurt me, T.J. wanted to say. But it wasn't Rusty she was thinking about now. She didn't want to want Nick DeSalvo. The fact that she did, whether it stemmed from chemistry, curiosity or perversion, hurt. Why hadn't she found some normal, nice guy to fall for? If she had, she wouldn't be so vulnerable to an attractive, intimidating man like Nick.

How could she ever overlook the fact that he'd killed her brother?

T.J. mustered her sarcasm to mask her fear. "Save it for your other women, DeSalvo."

"Other women?" He chuckled and T.J. felt the low, rough sound like a touch in the darkness. "Does that mean you're including yourself in my harem? In order to be a member you and I have to get a lot closer than we are now."

"Go to sleep. That's as close as we're going to get." T.J. turned away and stomped noisily back to her bed. As if she weren't worried that he'd march right up those stairs and turn teasing words into touching. If he did, she wasn't sure she'd be able to stop him, or herself. The darkness was making her a little crazy. In the morning things would look normal again. "Good night," she added as she pulled the sheet up to her neck and held her breath.

"Chicken." His voice still had that teasing quality, but somehow T.J. knew he wouldn't push her. She smiled into the shadows around her bed then caught herself. She didn't want to like Nick DeSalvo, either. Wanting him was bad enough.

THE EXPRESSION on Jackson's face when Nick opened the door the following morning was priceless.

"What are you doing here?" Jackson said looking over Nick's shoulder directly at T.J.

Nick answered the question. With his back to her, T.J. couldn't tell if he was smiling or not, but his voice sounded as if he were grinning. "None of your business."

Tyler, the building manager, pushed past Jackson but stopped at Nick. "T.J.?"

T.J. slid off the stool at the counter and moved to the door. She nudged Nick out of the way. "Come on in."

"I called the locksmith—" Tyler began to say, but Jackson interrupted.

"What the hell is going on, T.J.?" Jackson shut the door a little harder than necessary and crossed his arms. He surveyed Nick up and down, taking in his buttoned, but untucked, shirt and the coffee cup balanced in his hand. "I thought you wanted this guy out of here."

What she wanted had gotten totally lost in the shuffle somehow. T.J. experienced a moment of total exasperation and embarrassment. All three men stood waiting for her response. "If you must know, he stayed here last night."

Jackson's features settled into a harsher frown.

"After my purse and the key to the loft were stolen yesterday, I was afraid the thief might break in before I could get the locks changed. Nick . . ." She turned to face him and lost her train of thought. Smiling slightly, he stood there looking at her with a warm, indulgent gaze as if to say he would go along with whatever lie she wanted to tell. She felt like kicking him. "Stop it," she said, instead.

"What?" Nick acted surprised. "I didn't do anything."

"That's right—" she turned to Jackson "—he didn't do anything. He slept on the couch."

"It's none of his business what we do," Nick countered losing his indulgence.

"I said, stop it!" With that, T.J. decided to retire as referee. She took Tyler's arm and led him to the kitchen counter. "I need new locks and I guess we should talk to building security."

As T.J. filled Tyler in on some of the problems she'd been having, Nick and Jackson apparently lost interest in annoying each other. Jackson especially. She'd answered most of Nick's questions, but she knew Jackson wanted to ask about the one thing she could never tell Nick. *What was in the briefcase?* She hoped he wouldn't bring it up.

Tyler seemed so alarmed by her story that T.J. found herself having to comfort him instead of the other way around.

"This is terrible!" Tyler said. "I'm going to get on the phone and demand police protection for you."

"No," T.J. replied quickly and glanced at Nick. "No police. They can't help me with this."

"What do you mean they can't help?" Like a feisty terrier, Tyler wouldn't let it go. "Crimes have been committed and—"

"The police will do more harm than good," Nick cut in.

Tyler stopped sputtering and looked to Jackson for his support. Jackson remained silent but T.J. felt his eyes on her and had to fight the urge to squirm. She met his gaze and willed him *not* to ask the question on his mind—or mention her father. Not yet. Finally, he spoke. "If that's what you want, T.J. Just keep an eye on the place, Tyler." He walked back toward the door and put one large hand on the knob. "But—" he stared at them "—if anybody hurts T.J., I'm holding you responsible, DeSalvo." He opened the door and walked out.

There was one long silent moment in Jackson's wake, then Nick glanced at his watch. "Since Tyler's here and the locksmith's on the way...I have to run an errand," he said. He put his coffee cup down and moved to the table near the couch to pick up his wallet and car keys.

T.J. wasn't sure what to say to him, and she certainly didn't want to say anything with Tyler as an audience.

"Why don't you pour yourself a cup of coffee, Tyler?" She hoped that would keep him busy for a while.

A moment later, Nick was standing before her with his shirt tucked in, his coat over his arm and a guarded look on his face. He didn't say a word.

T.J. fell back on manners and realized that she owed him. The thought sent a chill through her but the truth was looking her in the eye. He'd protected her and he hadn't asked for a thing.

"Thank you," she said.

He just stared at her. Then one of his hands rose to tuck a strand of hair behind her ear. The intimacy of that gesture made heat rise to her face. Not only because Tyler might be watching, but because she'd wanted to turn and press her face to his palm. She held herself perfectly still.

"You're welcome," he said and dropped his hand. His eyes were dark and serious and he looked as if he wanted to kiss her. But he didn't.

"Lock your doors. I'll call you from work."

"Okay." T.J. agreed. Dealing with him on the phone was much easier than dealing with him in person. Especially when he looked at her as if he were waiting . . . for something. Something she'd never be able to give him.

"Bye," she said in a whisper.

"Remember what we talked about. No more pictures."

He didn't say goodbye.

"JACKSON, I CAN'T tell you everything. It would only put you in danger, too."

"Do you think I care about that? I know how to take care of myself. You're the one who needs a keeper!"

"Well, Nick is going to—"

"Nick! What do you know about him? I don't like the guy and the last time I checked, you didn't, either."

Jackson wasn't the type to dance around the issue. This time he'd stomped directly on her toe. "I, uh—I've changed my mind." He stared at her as if she'd *lost* her mind. "He used to be a cop and he—"

"Why did he quit?"

"He didn't exactly quit . . . he was fired."

"Great." He shook his head and sighed. He spoke slowly and distinctly, as if he were dealing with a ten-year-old child. "You don't get fired from the police force unless you've been accused of something illegal, unethical, or stupid. Now tell me how this guy can help you?"

Nick had fulfilled all three requirements when he'd killed her brother. T.J. flinched from the thought. Now the only way Nick could help her was to keep her safe long enough to present the evidence in the briefcase. By doing that, he'd be allowing her to prove his guilt in the conspiracy. She couldn't tell Jackson those facts and then expect him to say, "Fine, no problem."

"I need him to help me. He knows how the bad guys work," she said. But what she really needed was for Nick to be innocent. Impossible. "Besides, he's already involved." She moved closer to Jackson. "Thank you for giving a damn about me. I don't want you to think I don't appreciate it. But I can't ask you to do more than you're doing already. You're the only one I would trust with the briefcase."

"Then I can assume your fallen officer doesn't know what's in it, either?"

"Nobody knows."

He looked even more exasperated. "Why don't you go to a real cop, then?"

T.J. gazed into Jackson's questioning eyes and knew she had to tell him. She'd put him in danger, he had a right to know why. But she had a feeling that telling him would only increase the threat. Once the words were out, she couldn't take them back and Jackson wasn't the type to forget.

"The briefcase I gave you was hidden in my father's things. It contains evidence of a crime committed by several county police officers." She shrugged at the obvious dilemma. "And . . . I don't know which ones to trust."

WHEN THE INTERCOM buzzed early that evening, T.J. knew it was Nick. If she had any brains left at all she would pretend not to be here. Let him buzz until building security sent him on his way. But she couldn't do it. As much as it pained her to admit it, she wanted to see him.

Christmas Eve. Tomorrow she'd planned to celebrate the downfall of one ex-police officer named Nick DeSalvo. Instead, he'd invited himself to dinner at her loft with the excuse of keeping an eye on her. It was a pretty thin excuse. She had new locks on the doors, the undivided attention of the building manager and each shift of security, and she had no plans to go out. Yet she hadn't said no.

She pushed the button to answer the buzz. "Yes?"

"It's Nick. Hey, hurry up, I've got my hands full."

T.J. pushed the door release. *His hands full?* If he'd been silly enough to buy Christmas presents, she'd send him right back to the parking lot.

When she opened the door, she didn't know whether to laugh or cry. He'd brought a Christmas tree, albeit a small one, and had a brown paper sack balanced in the crook of his other arm.

"Ho, ho, ho?" he said as if he expected a fight.

T.J. just stared at him for several seconds then she stepped back to allow him in. He pushed the two-foot tree at her.

"Find a place for this, will you? I'll put the wine in the refrigerator."

Not knowing what else to do, T.J. took the small tree and settled it on the plant stand near the front windows. The tree was beautifully done by a florist or an artist—not something one would pick up at a department store. There were real dried flowers interspersed with greenery and tiny bows. The ornaments were all natural elements of wood or berries and the whole tree was laced with baby's breath, creating the effect of snow.

Nick came to stand beside her. "Sorry it doesn't have lights. You really should put some lights up. What will Georgia Power do without your contribution to their profits?"

She knew he was joking about the whole thing but she felt unaccountably touched. "It's lovely. Thank you."

"You sound surprised," he said.

"I am."

"Oh." He put a hand to his chest as if she'd wounded him. "You're a cruel woman."

She cocked an eyebrow at his uncharacteristic display. He shrugged and his mouth quirked but his expression turned serious. "It just looked like something you'd like." Before she could comment, he changed the subject. "What's for dinner?"

T.J. walked away before she did something foolish like touch him. She fought the crazy physical pull by shifting back to teasing. "I wouldn't be so eager if I were you. How do you know I can cook?"

He looked alarmed. "Can you?"

"You're about to find out—the hard way."

They ate dinner like two diplomats contemplating a peace treaty. T.J. was determined to get through it without thinking about the chasm of trouble between them and Nick seemed determined to convince her that he was on her side. The wine was cool, the chicken tasty and the atmosphere seemed calm and unthreatening. Until he made an innocuous comment about his former wife.

T.J. was surprised by the rush of turbulent emotion she felt at the thought of a woman living with Nick, loving him. And he, her.

"How long were you married?" she asked. She took a sip of wine to brace herself for the answer. Did she really want to know?

"Four years."

"What happened?" She wondered who had wanted out of the marriage. And who might still be in love.

He gave her a half smile. "Nothing sinister. I'd been on the Buffalo police force a couple of years when I met a cop from Florida. He made living in the South sound so good I decided to give it a try." Nick took a sip of his wine and shook his head. "Susan and I made it as far as Atlanta. It was spring and after surviving the winter in Buffalo, this place looked like heaven. I got a job with the county. My buddy Mike and his wife Gina moved down here, too. Things looked great.

"Six months later Susan started talking about going back home. She had no friends here, and couldn't seem to make any. I was working all the time and she felt alone without her family.

"So, she went."

"And you stayed," T.J. added.

He leaned back in his chair. "Yeah. I liked it here. So did Mike and Gina. Susan probably would have liked it, too, if she'd stayed long enough. It's funny—my best friend was willing to trust my judgment, but my wife wouldn't.

"I thought if I gave her some time, she'd come back. A year later, she divorced me and I married my job.

I've been here ever since. End of story." After only a slight pause he asked, "What about you?"

"Me?"

"Yeah." He pinned her with his gaze. "Ever been married?"

T.J. thought of all the times she'd wished for a normal life, to be married someday and settled down like many of her friends. But she hadn't been "normal" since her brother was killed. She couldn't tell that to the man who'd killed him, so she gave Nick an innocuous answer hoping he wouldn't push. "No. Oh, I date but nothing serious. I want to get my career going. You know."

"Anybody special?"

He looked perfectly at ease asking her the question. Only the absolute stillness of his hands and his body gave away his interest.

"I'm not a virgin, if that's what you want to know."

"That's part of what I want to know."

"Why? What difference does it make?"

"I don't seduce virgins."

"I see." T.J. pushed back from the table and picked up her empty dish and reached for his. "So that means you think you're going to seduce me."

He stopped her by placing a hand on her arm. "Only if that's what you want. It's definitely crossed my mind."

T.J. couldn't look into his dark, mesmerizing gaze. She hated herself for her body's reaction to his words, wanting to be seduced, regardless of the past or the future. She could barely speak. "I thought you were here to protect me."

"I'm here because I care about you. But wanting you goes along with that." He let go of her arm. "We're both adults. I can take no for an answer, but I won't sit here and pretend I'm not thinking about you...about us."

T.J. had no suitable reply because he'd voiced exactly what she'd been doing—pretending. She walked toward the sink to rinse the dishes. A moment later Nick moved next to her and handed her their empty wineglasses. "Hey, I didn't mean to ruin your whole night. I'm really harmless."

He looked about as harmless as a timber wolf lounging inside a barn full of sheep. As soon as he got hungry...all hell would break loose. T.J. tried to think of anything to turn the conversation away from the two of them. She blurted out the first thing that came to mind.

"If your friends Mike and Gina liked life here in Atlanta so much, why did he kill himself?"

Nick's expression turned hard and all the playfulness disappeared. The cruelty of her words tasted like acid on her tongue. Suddenly, she didn't like the bitter, vengeful person she'd become. "I'm sorry— I—"

He walked away.

T.J. quickly dried her hands and followed him into the living area. She found him staring out the windows at the moon-washed courtyard with his hands jammed in his pockets. She moved up behind him and reached out to touch him, but the forbidding set of his shoulders caused her to draw back.

"You didn't deserve that." She sighed. Before she could think of anything else to say, he spoke.

"Did I tell you that he killed himself on Christmas Eve?"

T.J. thought her heart would surely stop beating. The words vibrated with pain and anger. He had a right to be angry with her, she—

"I've made it a point to never be alone on Christmas Eve since then." He turned to look at her. "And I don't carry my weapon, in case it starts to look like a solution, like it did for Mike."

"I'm so sorry," T.J. managed to say. She fought the tears welling in her eyes. She felt as if she'd stabbed him in the chest. How did she ever think she could punish this man and feel good about it? No matter what he'd done in the past.

"I didn't want to be alone tonight. But if you don't want me here—"

"Stay." T.J. realized that she meant it. She wanted this night, even if tomorrow they became enemies. She'd wanted his head on a platter for Christmas, but this was Christmas Eve, and tonight they could still be allies. She rested her hand on his upper arm.

The living area was dark except for the two candles on the coffee table she'd lit earlier. The darkness suited her mood. Wanting this man was like staring into the abyss. It wasn't suicide, it was darker than that, and she couldn't fathom the outcome. But logic and reason were gone. She only knew how she felt.

T.J. stepped closer, ran her hand along his shoulder then upward until her palm rested against his cheek. His skin was hot and the slight roughness sent a shiver along her wrist and inner arm. As she raised her chin to offer her mouth, he resisted.

"I don't want your pity."

T.J. almost smiled. A dark bewitchment seemed to have taken control, forcing her to tell the truth. "Good, because I refuse to have any pity for you."

A flush of angry wildness went through Nick making him want to howl at the moon like a wild man. When would he ever stop facing the ghosts around him? Gazing at T.J., Nick felt as if he were holding a phantom in his arms, warm but insubstantial, likely to disappear any moment.

He looked down into T.J.'s dreamy, shadowed gaze and knew he'd be different after this night. He could see the warning in her eyes, feel the uncertainty inside himself. His future, however it turned out, would be affected by this woman. But nothing could make him walk away. *If I should die before I wake* . . . He lowered his mouth to hers and accepted his fate.

8

T.J.'S MOUTH TREMBLED under his, but instead of slowing down he pressed harder, delved deeper. He'd show her there was nothing to be afraid of—for either of them. He'd kiss her and touch her and make her quake from need instead of nervousness. Then he'd give her what she needed, what they'd both needed since that day on the street.

He shifted T.J. until her back was to the window then he pulled her closer. In the process, he bumped the stupid Christmas tree and had to catch it before it fell. He set it upright with his left hand then brought his gaze back to the woman in his arms.

He looked down into her eyes and saw the heat he wanted to see. He saw another emotion, too. She wasn't backing down but he could see a sadness in her shadowed green eyes, some dark memory or pain. The sight of it caused his fingers to flex and his hands to automatically tighten to hold her steady.

Then he kissed her again. Blotting out the thought of Mike and guilt, and whether or not he was dreaming. He wanted the sweetness, the warmth of T.J. He wanted to be skin to skin—even closer. He wanted all of her, tonight.

"Invite me up those stairs—" he managed to say, pulling his mouth away for a moment. She didn't answer and he pressed her with his lips. Then he purposely ran his hands up the sides of her blouse, almost to her breasts but stopped just short.

"Say it. Say you want me in your bed."

She angled her chin upward until her warm breath caressed his ear. He waited several seconds. She was so still that he thought she'd changed her mind. That she would push him away and ask him to leave. He didn't know if he could do it—let her go and walk away. He hoped for both their sakes she wouldn't ask. He'd never felt so out of control, not anywhere near as harmless as he claimed.

"I want you in my bed."

The words were low, and said in a rush, but Nick didn't care. In relief, he loosened his embrace, took her hand and led her to the stairs.

Even when T.J. felt the back of her legs bump the bed, it still didn't seem real. Being in Nick's arms, having his mouth make love to hers, his tongue stroking, sucking. A wave of dizziness struck, she couldn't seem to catch her breath. She pulled away from the kiss, gripped the loosened front of Nick's shirt and simply held on.

He went still except for his hands which slowed into a comforting slide up her spine. "You okay?" he mumbled into her hair.

"I can't breathe," she whispered then drew in as much air as possible with her face pressed against his neck. He smelled new, yet so familiar, so male. Her body was on fire for him but the fear, the guilt was strangling her. He shifted her away to look into her eyes.

"Whatever it is, put it away for tonight." He kissed her gently on the nose. "Just one night."

T.J. looked into Nick's dark questioning eyes and saw raw need. He needed her as much as she needed him. She closed her eyes and inwardly apologized to her father and Rusty. Tonight she wanted Nick, desperately, and she couldn't let him go. Just for tonight.

She immediately felt lighter. If denial was her only excuse, then so be it. For right now, she would be a woman without a past filled with pain. A woman who was about to make love to a perfect stranger. Man and woman. Chemistry and hormones. Need and fulfillment.

With a slight smile, she loosened her grip on his shirt and began to loosen the buttons. "For tonight," she said softly, then pulled the tail of his shirt from the waistband of his pants.

His skin was hot enough to warm the cool air in her loft. Soon, with his help, she was bare to the waist and the feel of his chest against the sensitive peaks of her breasts sent a tightening shiver of pleasure through her belly. She'd been with two other lovers in the past, but the memories seemed childish and pale compared to Nick.

Everything about him seemed dark. The heated promise of sensuality in his eyes, the springy hair on his chest and stomach that teased her nipples . . . his silence. She had his complete concentration and the pull of it held her immobile as he led her toward what they both wanted.

Nick flipped back the covers on the bed and lowered her until she was lying flat, looking up at him. He deftly unfastened her slacks and nudged her to raise her hips so he could remove them. He left her panties in place. Then, while she watched, he stripped out of his slacks, taking underwear along with them. He stared down at her for a moment, gloriously nude, and T.J. was fascinated. Not purely by the shape and the fitness of his body, but by his reaction to her gaze. She could still see the darkness in him, and the darkness wanted her to look at him, to see his arousal, to know how much he wanted her.

T.J. felt a rush of heat as a blush rose to warm her face and chest. As if he could see her reaction in the shadows, he moved over her, balancing his weight on his arms but covering her from head to toe.

He looked into her eyes for several seconds, then, as she watched, he lowered his head and took one pouting nipple between his lips. He sucked lightly then laved it with his tongue before blowing a puff of cool air on it. T.J. gasped and her nipple tightened to a straining peak.

"Are you ready for this?" he asked, but before she could answer, he gave her other nipple the same treatment. He moved back to the first before he asked, "Hmmm?" The vibration made T.J.'s toes curl and she moved her legs restlessly. She'd forgotten the question.

"Yes," she breathed. Yes to anything, to everything.

"If I do something you don't like—" he sucked again, a bit harder "—you tell me."

T.J. could only concentrate on his tongue and the fire shooting from her nipple to the core of her, as if his mouth had found both places at once.

"And, if I don't do something you want me to do—" he bit her nipple hard enough to make her jump "—tell me that, too."

T.J. didn't care what he was saying. She wanted him to stop talking. She framed his face with her hands and drew him up to kissing level. His mouth took hers completely, almost brutally, as if by inviting him, she'd given him carte blanche.

The night shifted, grew darker, more intimate. Nick loomed over her, the warm weight of him pressed her down. Instead of being afraid, T.J. experienced a feeling of rightness, of inevitability. They'd both been wounded, they both needed comfort. Why not with each other, why not tonight? She met him halfway, moving her hands along the taut muscles of his shoulders and back. Her fingers brushed the rough texture of a scar. Her palm barely covered it and T.J. knew from the size and the position that it had been a serious injury. Nick pulled back from the kiss.

"I promise you won't regret this," he whispered close to her ear. Then he pressed his damp lips to her neck.

T.J. slid her hand away from the scar and wondered how he'd read her fears. She *knew* she'd regret this but had made up her mind to take something for herself tonight. She wanted to be past the point of thought. She didn't want to know he'd been hurt, maybe nearly killed. She wouldn't allow mental images of death and pain to intrude, to hold her in the past. When he bit her shoulder then licked the same stinging spot, her mind went blank and her body took over. She bit him back.

The low, sexy sound of Nick's chuckle sent a hot spasm of pleasure through her. "Come on, let's play." He pushed downward, stopping briefly to tease her nipples in the same fashion as before. Then he moved lower.

T.J. could feel his hot breath on her belly and fought the urge to raise her hips. His fingers lightly traced the outside of her thighs . . . then moved to the inside. He coaxed her legs wider apart but didn't touch her. Investigating the top edge of her panties with his fingers as if he weren't sure how they stayed on or came off, he ran one finger along the elastic inner edge, then downward.

T.J. gasped and tried not to move.

Nick smiled to himself. Everything about T.J. made him crazy. The warm whisper of her breath, the smooth texture of her skin, the trembling readiness in her muscles. He wanted to know all her secrets. He lowered his head and lightly nuzzled the silken panties covering her most intimate physical secret.

He felt the sharpness of her fingernails as she gripped his shoulders and waited for a heartbeat to see if she'd stop him. He knew he was going way too fast, pushing too hard. But something drove him, something beyond the urgency of physical release. He was caught up in the idea that he had to hold her any way he could because she wasn't his, she might never be his . . . except for tonight.

When T.J. didn't stop him, he breathed a sigh of relief. Then with one finger, he began working her panties downward.

Nick used his mouth and his tongue to convince her that what they were doing was right. He wanted this Christmas Eve to be one she'd never forget, one that could replace both of their dark memories. He continued to taste and tease and by the time he heard her moan softly and felt her hips shift restlessly under his hands, Nick was nearly mindless himself. He wanted to continue, to send her over the edge but his body had other ideas. He was so hard . . . and she was so hot.

"Please . . ." T.J.'s plea seemed lost, distant. Yet she was beneath him, warm and moist, and pulling him closer. He raised himself until he could take her mouth with his own, until the sensitive tip of his erection prodded the secret folds his tongue had tasted.

"Please . . ." She sighed again, and he plunged inside her.

T.J. gasped as he filled her. One of his hands slid beneath her and pulled her hips up to meet the next thrust. She wanted to help, to give as much as she was getting but the pleasure was so strong she felt stunned, immobilized. The best she could do was curl into him, open to him, and hold on.

He kissed her face, her neck, then moved down to tease and suckle one nipple. She finally understood what *being taken* meant. Nick had taken control of her body and in return she received the hot, scintillating pleasure of his mouth, his plunging thrusts. Another woman might have begged or screamed, or even whispered love words. T.J. felt release rising from the depths of her in the form of a shuddering, shaking moan. Then Nick's mouth was on hers, sucking in the sound of her pleasure as if he needed the taste of it, the feel of it on his tongue.

He thrust harder and faster until the moan became his own as he drove for completion. After one last powerful stroke, he collapsed against her, his head resting on her collarbone.

T.J. could feel every inch of him, inside and out. He was heavy but she didn't care. She raised one hand and curled it around the back of his neck and into his damp hair. If she died right here, with his warm weight holding her down, she'd be content. Then she wouldn't have to face herself in the morning.

Sluggishly one of his hands moved along her shoulder then upward to rest against her cheek. His thumb traced a path over her lips. "I told you it wouldn't hurt," he whispered.

The threat of tears made T.J. close her eyes. It was still Christmas Eve. She didn't have to regret anything until tomorrow. She kissed the top of his head. "No. It didn't hurt."

He pushed up then, to kiss her on the mouth. "Good. Because I have a few other things I'd like to try."

NICK OPENED HIS EYES and tried to make sense out of what he was seeing. A railing. Beyond that air. Stairs . . . T.J.'s. He rolled over to touch her, to remind them both that he was in her bed, but she was gone. He sat up and listened. There were no lights on downstairs, no sounds. He rubbed a hand over his eyes and back through his hair. The air felt colder, as if a door had been left open.

Suddenly alert, Nick pushed to the edge of the bed and reached for his clothes. Where the hell was she? As he stood to pull on his pants he noticed the trapdoor at the top of the stairs was slightly ajar. Quietly he went up the stairs and shoved the door a little wider. T.J. sat huddled in one corner of the balcony, dressed in a pair of sweatpants and a down jacket, her arms wrapped around her knees. Why was she sitting outside in the cold? In the dark? He went back to the bed, pulled the comforter off and dragged it with him up the stairs.

She didn't turn when he stepped onto the balcony, or speak when he wrapped part of the comforter around her and sat down beside her. When he leaned close to kiss the side of her face, she pulled away slightly.

All his inner alarms were going off, telling him that T.J. was about to say something he didn't want to hear. Gone was the warm and willing partner he'd made love to most of the night. The woman next to him was too still, too tense and Nick had a bad feeling about it.

He tried to keep his voice casual. "Can't sleep?"

"I had a nightmare. I was being stalked by Santa." The words were too toneless to make the wisecrack work.

He slid one hand over her cold fingers. "Why don't you come inside? You'll freeze out here."

T.J. didn't stand up. She merely loosened her hands and circled her fingers around his right wrist. She turned his hand over and held it still as she placed her left hand next to his, palm to palm. When she met his gaze he could see she had tears in her eyes.

Nick curled his fingers around hers tightly and held on. "What is it?" He sucked in a draft of cold air and a chill ran through him.

T.J. simply looked at him while silvery trails of moisture stained her cheeks. The look in her eyes made his chest hurt. He wanted to pull her closer but she didn't look as if she'd let him. "Tell me," he coaxed.

T.J. wanted to say, "It's not your fault." But it was his fault. The same strong, warm hand that held hers so tightly had also held the gun that killed her brother. Two and a half years before at the inquiry, Nick had admitted that much. Neither he nor she could change the outcome of his actions.

But it was her fault he'd gotten so close to her. Her fault that she'd actually wanted him to touch her, to love her. Now what could she say to him other than, go away. *I can never let this happen, ever again.* What would her father have to say if he could see her now?

"I uh..." She trained her blurred vision on the skyline in the distance. "I miss my dad. You know, Christmas and everything. He always made a big deal about Christmas." So much had happened in the past few weeks she hadn't had time to dwell on the fact that this was her first Christmas alone. Truth to tell she hadn't wanted to think about it. "This is the first year... He died in February."

"What about sisters or brothers?"

T.J. felt an inner chill that made the winter air around her seem balmy. "No. Just me."

"T.J., I—"

She put her fingers to his lips to stop him. She didn't want his understanding or his sympathy. "I'm just confused and scared and... tired." As she said the words, she realized all of it was true. "Very tired," she added and closed her eyes.

Nick tugged her closer and put his arms around her. "Come back to bed." He squeezed her gently. "To sleep. I'll keep you warm." He waited a moment for her answer, then stood, pulling her with him. She allowed him to guide her back down the stairs to her own bed—and her own bad dreams.

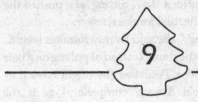

9

T.J. AWOKE TO the smells and sounds of bacon frying and coffee perking. She stretched and rolled to one side to see the digital clock on the night table. Nine-thirty. The last thing she remembered from the night before was Nick settling her against him. She'd slept like a worn-out child. She moved again and felt a tenderness between her legs. The vivid memory of Nick bending over her, moving inside her brought back the heat he'd ignited so effortlessly the night before.

She didn't want to go downstairs and face him. The night was over, which meant so was the truce. She couldn't pretend he was a sexy stranger. She knew too many things about him, like how his touch could shift from tender to demanding, how his mouth could coax and tease, how he could draw her out with sighs and promises and make her lose control.

But in the light of day, she had to acknowledge another more hurtful thing about him. One she could never forget. He'd killed her brother.

Her stomach rumbled, interrupting her dark thoughts. Life went on. She'd learned that lesson two and a half years ago. She had to face him, and right then, to her surprise, she felt hungry enough to bite first and ask questions later. Sitting, she pushed the covers back and headed for the shower.

"Good morning," she said twenty minutes later as she moved down the stairs. Instead of pulling on a pair of sweatpants and a T-shirt as she might have normally done, she'd dressed completely—as if she planned to go out. Or as if she had a stranger in her home.

Nick looked up from the stove, and T.J. felt the warmth of his gaze like a caress. "Merry Christmas."

T.J. almost missed a step. She'd forgotten Christmas along with her plans to celebrate Nick DeSalvo's just deserts as her only gift. And there he stood barefoot and half-dressed, the man she was supposed to destroy, cooking breakfast for her. There was something insidiously funny about the situation, but at that particular moment, T.J. couldn't appreciate it.

"Same to you," she managed to reply with a half smile. To avoid his eyes, she blazed a straight path to the coffeemaker and busied herself pouring a cup. When she glanced his way he was staring at her in a speculative way with a spatula balanced in his hand. "What are you making?" she asked to divert that questioning gaze.

His eyes held her captive for a few more seconds then shrugged. "The only breakfast food I know how to make...pancakes. I was starving and you were still asleep. I found everything I needed except maple syrup." He paused to slide a golden brown pancake from the pan onto a plate then handed it to her. "The bacon is on the counter."

T.J. turned automatically and stopped short. He'd gone through her kitchen like an invading army. There were bowls and measuring cups and at least twelve different spoons in the sink. Circles of pancake batter looked like crop rings left by aliens. "You must have a live-in maid," she said in awe of his complete disregard for whoever had to clean up after him.

He laughed in an easy, deprecating way. "I can't seem to cook without using every dish I find. Don't worry, I know how to load a dishwasher."

Suddenly T.J. was grateful for the chaos. Her kitchen, her life, had been in perfect order for too long. And this was one mess that could be cleaned up in thirty minutes or so. Not like the other more sinister chaos that had turned her into a target.

T.J. confessed to not having any syrup, so they made do with strawberry jam. They ate breakfast like two people who had made love all night and needed to refuel. Two people with so many unspoken words between them that eating breakfast seemed like the safest course.

A short time later Nick pushed his empty plate away and raised his coffee cup for a sip. He'd watched T.J.'s morning-after wariness long enough. He needed to know how she felt about the night before. He couldn't wait any longer.

"How are you feeling?" he asked, hoping she wouldn't say fine.

She swallowed the last bite of her food then stared at him for a moment. Her hand moved to her coffee cup and her fingers gripped the handle. "Fine," she said, finally.

Nick put down his cup and rested his forearms on the table. He felt like an actor confined to a civilized, delicate social situation that required patience and finesse when every muscle inside him wanted to stand, pull T.J. to her feet and kiss her until she melted. Like she'd done the night before.

"Just fine?" He tried not to sound disappointed.

She retreated for a few seconds, dropping her gaze to the cup caught between her two hands. When she looked up again she made a valiant attempt at a smile. Her eyes were absolutely serious. "I'm— I feel a little awkward."

She looked as if she'd been sentenced to the electric chair. He slid one hand over hers. Her skin felt cool, not warm and welcoming like it had the last time he'd touched her. "I hope you're not regretting what happened between us, because I certainly don't." He held his breath as he waited for her reaction.

T.J.'s eyes filled with tears, and Nick experienced that sinking, numb feeling he experienced when he'd been shot, but this time it felt closer to the heart. He tugged her hand away from the coffee cup and held her palm against his cheek. "Don't," he said, unable to think about his own pain after making her cry. "I didn't mean to—"

"It's okay," T.J. said as she rubbed her other hand across her cheek to wipe away the tears. "I uh— I just get emotional on holidays. And last night . . ."

Nick's fingers laced with hers so she couldn't pull her hand back. He required her touch in order to hear what she had to say.

"Last night—" she swallowed hard, fighting the tears "—we both needed someone."

Well, there you have it, folks—the truth. He almost sighed in resignation. She was right. They'd both needed someone for the night. But during those hours in the dark, Nick had found out he wanted a lot more than just a night from T.J. He didn't want to force the issue now. He also wasn't ready to leave and hope for the best.

"How about today?" he asked.

"What?" T.J. tugged her hand back and picked up her napkin to finish wiping her eyes.

"I promised I'd visit Gina and my goddaughter today. Go with me?"

"Oh, I don't think so, I—"

"Hey, it's Christmas and Christmas is for kids. Come on, don't stay here alone. We'll be your family today. I promise, when you're ready to leave, I'll bring you back." He waited for a few seconds before adding the unvarnished truth. "I want you to go."

She waited so long to answer, he was sure she'd concoct a wonderful excuse. He shifted in his chair, again fighting the urge to touch her.

T.J. didn't have to wonder why Nick wanted her to go with him. She could see it in his expression. A warm cascade of feeling seeped through her guilt. He wanted her with him, not as a trophy of conquest or part of some self-assigned protection plan, but as a friend—as a lover. She hadn't considered that possibility before; that he might truly care for her. It almost made her cry again.

God, she was so confused. Here was the man, the stranger she had hated for so long, looking at her...lovingly. And worse than that, part of her wanted him to look at her that way. Part of her wanted to bask in his sultry gaze like a naked sun lover on a deserted Hawaiian beach.

And what about her brother? What about the truth? She couldn't hide it forever. No matter how much she wanted to at that moment. When Nick found out her real name and what she had hidden at Jackson's, he wouldn't look at her with warmth ever again.

"I'll drive and have you back here by six o'clock. What do you say?" Nick was anything if not persistent.

"But they aren't expecting me," T.J. stalled, still trying to find some emotional balance. Her mind flashed back to the photographs of Gina from the demonstration. Officer Gina Tarantino, the person she'd originally wanted to talk with. Would it matter if she spoke to her now? She'd already found Nick— he'd practically taken over her life. Did she need to find the truth in Gina's eyes? Was she one of the bad cops like her husband?

"We'll have to stop at my place on the way. I need to change clothes and pick up their presents. I'll call her from there, but I'm sure she won't mind."

T.J. knew for a certainty that she'd stepped into the fire. She decided she might as well walk on through. "Okay."

The pleased look on Nick's face was almost worth the turmoil raging inside her. He didn't dwell on it, however. He stood and started squaring away the kitchen he'd trashed.

NICK'S TOWN HOUSE complex was twenty minutes north of downtown and a far cry from the urbane hipness of the Coach Works. As they stopped at the iron gate so Nick could insert his resident identification card, the man in the security booth gave a friendly wave. Everyone who knew Nick seemed to trust him. Everyone except T.J.

They parked in a covered garage. Nick walked around to open her door, but she opened it first and got out. Her action left her standing face-to-face with Nick. He caught the doorframe with one hand and leaned his other shoulder against the truck effectively trapping her. T.J.'s only option to avoid him was to duck under his arm. Instead, when he leaned toward her she drew in a breath, waiting for him to kiss her, wanting him to make her forget her confusion and doubt about his motives, and about her own.

His mouth was millimeters from hers when a car pulled in the garage one space down. Nick turned to face the sound as if he expected a Mafia hit. After a few tense seconds, he nodded and waved to one of his neighbors. Then he swore under his breath, took her arm, drew her forward and slammed the truck door. T.J. might have smiled another time, but right then, she'd wanted that kiss as much as Nick had. She'd wanted a taste of what they'd shared the evening before. With each hour that passed she felt the physical gap between them widening. As if they could turn back into strangers if they stayed apart long enough.

Nick unlocked the dead bolt on his front door and stepped inside to turn off the security system. T.J. followed him but stopped near the door.

"Make yourself at home," Nick said as he tossed his keys on the open counter dividing the kitchen from the dining room. He ran a hand over his chin and grimaced. "I'm going to take a quick shower and shave. I'll only be a few minutes."

T.J. stepped farther into the living room and looked around. A decorator had obviously chosen most of the furnishings. The effect was tasteful with dark woods and hunter green leather. A large entertainment center took up most of one wall. The room looked comfortable and chic, yet she couldn't see Nick's personality.

She walked around the couch toward what looked like an enclosed sunporch. It turned out to be Nick's office. This was where he really lived, she decided as she moved into the room. Sunlight streamed through the windows. A computer station complete with bookshelves had been built into the far corner. Next to it sat a sleek desk made of dark mahogany that any corporate executive might admire, littered with papers and files and flanked by matching filing cabinets. The wall behind the desk was crowded with pictures and framed awards. Nearly every person in the photos wore a uniform.

T.J.'s heart began to pound. She stared at one photo of a younger, happier Nick in uniform, smiling, standing next to another policeman. *This is who he is*, her inner voice whispered. *A cop.* She'd put that fact out of her mind, conveniently forgetting that he'd spent years wearing a uniform, that his best friends were cops, that he used to carry a gun.

He still carried a gun.

Her thoughts zigzagged back to the day they'd been shot at on the street. He'd had a gun then. She wondered where it had been last night. She hadn't found it as she'd undressed him. The memory of being in Nick's arms, of completely losing herself in the touch of him, the taste of him, literally made her knees weak.

"It figures you'd end up in the messiest room in the place," Nick said.

Startled, T.J. turned to find him standing in the doorway behind her. Her breath caught. He was wearing a pair of pressed navy Dockers but hadn't put on a shirt yet. His chest was bare except for the towel draped around his neck.

"I'm always interested in pictures," she said and pivoted back to the array on the wall. She felt him move up behind her and the same sweet lethargy from a moment before made her want to lean back, to feel his chest against her. She tried to distract them both.

She pointed to a picture of Nick with Gina and another policeman. "Is that your friend who . . . died? Gina's husband?" Logically, she'd known the answer before she'd asked the question, but she needed to say something to defuse the fact that they were alone in his apartment, he was half-dressed and looking good enough to eat. Memories of his mouth, his hands moving over her skin, holding her down, caused an immediate reaction inside her. She felt her skin growing warmer.

As if he'd read her mind, his hands ran up her arms from elbow to shoulder. Firm and steady, the first time he'd intentionally touched her since he'd briefly held her hand at breakfast. "Yes," he answered but he wasn't looking at the picture. He brushed back her hair so that his lips were near her ear. "I'm trying to be a gentleman here," he said in a low tone that made the hair at the back of her neck tingle.

He smelled of soap and shaving cream, and she could imagine how his skin would taste, clean and damp from the shower. "What do you mean?" she asked but couldn't stop herself from drawing in another deep breath and tilting her head to give him better access to her neck.

"Well, what I want to do is turn you around and bend you back over this desk."

T.J. closed her eyes as his mouth made a wet trail along her throat. She'd gone this far. Saying no when she wanted to say yes seemed childish. The hinges had been blown off that barn door. "So, what's stopping you?"

It was obviously not the answer he'd expected. He abandoned the sensual torture he'd been lavishing on her neck and rotated her in his arms. He stared down into her eyes for several long seconds. What he saw seemed to please him because one side of his mouth slanted up in a sexy, knowing smile. He lowered his mouth and breathed the answer against her lips. "I can be a gentleman long enough to make it to the couch." Then instead of kissing her, he bent and picked her up.

Nick settled T.J. on the couch and sat down beside her. He gazed into her sea green eyes as he pulled the towel from around his neck and dropped it to the floor. He felt like grinning at his good fortune, but then it occurred to him that there were other, better suited things for his mouth to be doing just then.

Caging her with his arms, he kissed and teased her lips until she made that small sound he'd heard the night before. The sigh of surrender, or of need, that sent a shiver of response straight through him. He'd never get tired of hearing that sound. He deepened the kiss, plunging farther, demanding more from her.

She didn't disappoint him. Her hands were on his chest moving, smoothing, stopping to tease his nipples. Even with his logic halfway off-line he realized she intended to turn the tables. Intended to push him as he'd pushed her the night before. That was fine as far as Nick was concerned. He wasn't a chauvinist. Let the lady do what she wanted as long as she wanted to do it with him.

He pulled away from her mouth and went to work on the buttons of her blouse. She ran her tongue along the edge of his ear then bit his earlobe. Her mouth was dangerous, he knew that already. With a groan, he covered her lips with his own.

Between the two of them they managed to get naked. As Nick slid over the length of the woman lying bare on his leather couch, he had to stop and savor the moment. He remembered being in this position in the middle of the street during the demonstration. At that time he'd only noticed the softness of a female body and felt the hard edge of her anger. Why hadn't he seen how beautiful she was?

He could see it now. As he stared down at the pink flush tinting her skin and her face, at her mouth, moist and slightly swollen from his kisses, and her long blond hair fanned out over the smooth leather, he knew he was in big trouble. But along with that realization came the thought that he didn't want it any other way. He'd always been attracted to trouble.

Nick trapped T.J.'s face between his hands and kissed her as tenderly as he knew how. He wanted to tell her he'd never hurt her, that he'd always keep her safe, but his ego wasn't sure she wouldn't laugh. So he looked for permission in her eyes. He drew back and watched her face as he slowly entered her, his hardness straining deep into her liquid softness.

The leather of the couch creaked softly and he felt T.J. take a deep breath. And then he saw it, the tiny spark of tenderness, of welcome in her eyes. She wanted him, not the next guy or the last one. She wanted Nick DeSalvo.

THE RED-AND-GREEN Christmas wreath on Gina Tarantino's front door hung at an odd angle, as if it had been knocked to the ground and replaced in a hurry. Nick pushed the doorbell and called out, "Ho, ho, ho. Merry Christmas!"

The door seemed to fly open and Gina along with two children crowded into the opening. The wreath hit the ground near T.J.'s feet. Nick bent over to receive a hug from a little girl who had to be his goddaughter, Emma, and T.J. picked up the Christmas decoration.

"Hi. Welcome," Gina said looking at T.J. rather than Nick. "Come on in." Her gaze dropped to the wreath. "Oh, just—"

"Uncle Nick, you brought presents!" Emma squealed.

"Yes, I brought presents," Nick replied. "But I want to see what Santa brought you." The two little girls made an abrupt about-face and pelted down the hallway toward the living room.

T.J. returned the wreath to a semistraight position on its hook. "I hope you don't mind my being here. I told Nick—"

"Mind? Absolutely not. The more the merrier I've always thought." She waved a hand. "Please come in out of the cold." She shut the door behind them. "The house is in total chaos. I hope you can stand a little clutter. We have Christmas paper and ribbons from one end of the room to the other. Sometimes I think six-year-olds like playing with the paper and the boxes more than they like the actual presents."

She leaned up to kiss Nick on the cheek. "So, how are you this fine Christmas morning?" she asked with a conspiratorial smile.

"I'm excellent," he replied without returning the smile. "How are you doing?"

"Good," Gina said. When Nick seemed unconvinced, she added, "Really, I'm good." She shoved one shoulder. "Go in and put those presents down before the holy terrors return and demand to open them."

They moved into the living room and Nick knelt next to the Christmas tree to unload the presents in his arms. The whole process was watched with great interest by Emma and her friend. As Nick stood up and returned to sit with T.J. on the couch, Emma nearly tackled her mother by throwing her arms around her knees.

"Can we open presents now?"

Gina smiled sheepishly at T.J. and Nick. "I think there was too much sugar in that breakfast cereal I gave her this morning." She looked down at her daughter. "Wait a minute. There's something we have to do first." Gina took both Emma and her friend by the hand and brought them to stand in front of the couch. "Okay, say hello and Merry Christmas to T.J. and Nick." The girls piped up in unison except that Emma added uncle to Nick.

"All right, now. T.J.? This is Emma." She put a hand on her daughter's head. "And this is Courtney. Courtney is Emma's best friend in the world. Right Emma?" Emma nodded. "Courtney's mother had to work today so she's staying with us for Christmas."

After the introductions were complete, Gina offered T.J. and Nick coffee, which they declined. With the formalities out of the way she moved to present opening.

"Emma, get Uncle Nick's present."

T.J. watched Nick make a great fuss over the beautiful wrapping paper on his present. It had obviously been put together by Emma because she'd chosen two different colors. She smiled proudly when he asked who wrapped it so well.

When he opened the box, T.J. had to stifle a laugh. It was the funniest, most appropriate present Emma could have picked out for Nick DeSalvo, hater of ties. Nick reverently pulled the tie from the box and shook his head in amazement. "A tie with—" He looked at it more closely.

"With Jerry Garcia on it," Gina finished for him.

Nick gave her a pained look before he smiled at Emma. "It's perfect, sweetheart. Just what I wanted." He opened his arms to Emma and she gave him a hug. He kissed her on the cheek. "Thank you, honey."

Gina rolled her eyes for T.J.'s benefit. "Put it on, Uncle Nick," she added with an evil grin.

"Maybe later," he said placing the tie back in the box.

"No," Emma interrupted. "Put it on now, Uncle Nick." She pushed the tie into his hand. "Please?"

"Okay, but this isn't the right shirt for a great tie like this." Without looking at either Gina or T.J., he flipped the tie around his neck and began tying it.

Sometime after the traditional Christmas dinner with an Italian addition—pasta—T.J. finally began to feel comfortable being in Gina's home. She seemed so different from the all-business police officer T.J. had met on the street. With her daughter she was like any other loving mother, any other single parent. The only clue to her profession came in the pointed humor she wielded at Nick.

T.J. wondered how a household that seemed so normal on the surface could have been the center of so many dark secrets. Had these two people planned and executed her brother as she had supposed only a week ago? It didn't seem possible. Her eyes settled on Nick again. She couldn't stop looking at him.

Seated in the middle of the floor, he was helping Emma put together the dollhouse he'd brought her.

With their heads together Emma and Nick inserted tab A into slot B and the house took form. As they arranged the furniture and unwrapped the green plastic bushes to go next to the front door, Emma changed the subject abruptly.

"Uncle Nick? I asked Santa to bring me a daddy but he didn't."

T.J. glanced at Gina and she seemed frozen in place. Nick looked into his goddaughter's upturned, unhappy face and T.J. held her breath.

"Well, sweetie. Maybe he couldn't find the right one yet. Maybe he'll bring one next year."

Emma gravely handed Nick the toy car to put in the attached garage of her dollhouse. "Will you be my daddy?"

One of Nick's large hands brushed back Emma's hair. Witnessing the gentleness of Nick's touch, T.J. couldn't imagine his hand, the same hand that had touched her in passion, had ever held the gun that killed her brother.

"I can't, Em. A daddy is someone special, someone both you and your mommy love."

"We love you," Emma continued in a smaller voice.

"I know you do. And I love both of you. But a daddy is different...." For the first time, Nick looked to Gina for help.

Gina walked over and hugged her daughter before tickling her into a giggling fit. "Uncle Nick can't be your daddy, silly. He's your uncle."

Gasping for breath, Emma squealed, "Yes he can!"

"No, he can't!"

"Yes—he—can—" Emma was out of breath but still smiling.

Gina gave Nick an exasperated shake of her head. "I think she's been talking to Grandma again. Everyone called today—my mother, my sister and all three of my brothers. Each of them has a nice man they want me to meet. I'm sure it's pure coincidence that every one of those *nice* men live in Buffalo."

She gave her daughter another playful squeeze then nudged her forward. "Now, give *Uncle* Nick a hug and thank him for your dollhouse."

"Thank you, Uncle Nick," Emma said and planted a wet kiss on his cheek.

"You're welcome," Nick replied as he hugged her tight.

T.J. met Gina's gaze and thought her heart would break. How could a woman who'd gone through the loss of a husband allow anyone to murder a teenage boy? The image wouldn't fit.

And what about Nick? She'd just watched him protect the child he loved the best way he knew how. How could this man have cold-bloodedly killed Rusty?

Nick pushed to his feet, giving up his position in front of the dollhouse and glancing at his watch. Then his eyes met T.J.'s. "It's about time for us to hit the road," he said.

T.J. stood. "Yes, I guess we should get going." She turned to Gina and extended her hand. "Thank you for dinner. It was nice to see you again," she said, falling back on manners. She didn't know if she was happy to know that Gina couldn't be a murderer or if she'd wanted to witness the darkness she'd believed in for so long. T.J.'s plan to talk to Gina and find out what happened the night her brother died went as flat as a punctured tire. Alone or in a crowd, Gina would never say anything to hurt Nick. That much had been made perfectly clear.

"Yeah, thanks, kid. Dinner was great," Nick agreed.

"You're welcome," Gina replied. She kissed Nick on the cheek again, then looked at T.J. "I hope you know this is one of the good guys."

T.J. could only nod and try to hide the pain in her heart. As for T.J.'s enemy, her lover, Nick DeSalvo, everything had gotten so confused between them she didn't know what to believe anymore.

10

"SHOULD I STAY, or go?" Nick asked. He'd already given the loft a security check another policeman might admire. "I don't like the thought of you here alone."

The sun had set as they'd driven back to the Coach Works. T.J. had returned home to find a note on her door inviting her to a Christmas party at Jackson's that evening and an answering machine jammed by hang-ups. She tossed the note and unplugged the machine.

She needed time. Clear-thinking time, away from everyone. Especially Nick. She couldn't give in to the purely selfish wish to keep him close enough to touch. "I've been living in this loft for months by myself."

"That was before you took it upon *yourself* to investigate the county police."

She hated being thought of as helpless, especially since her reason for being in this mess was the man asking the questions. If it wasn't for Nick DeSalvo, her life would be a giant step closer to normal right now. "The locks have been changed. I have a security system, and Jackson close by." When Nick frowned she impulsively added, "I also have a gun if I need it."

That got his attention. She should have known better. Instead of backing off, he took a step forward. "What kind of gun?"

"A nine millimeter something or other. I have bullets, too. So, you see, I'm perfectly fine here—"

"Do you know how to fire it?"

"Well, I—"

"Do you know how many people are shot with their own weapons? Where do you keep it?"

"In my darkroom."

"What good would it do you in there if someone breaks in? Go get it."

T.J.'s first impulse was to refuse. The fact that he kept interrupting her was enough to make her rebel. Not to mention that this particular gun was part of the evidence she didn't want Nick to know about yet.

He must have seen mutiny on her face. He sighed and ran a hand through his hair. "Look, just show me you know how to handle it properly and I'll leave. Guns are serious business."

A gun is a gun, T.J. wavered. The man at the gun shop where she'd bought the bullets had said that nine millimeters were fairly common. She wouldn't have to explain where she got it; she could tell Nick she'd bought it used in the shop. The sooner he saw it, the sooner he'd leave and she could try to pull herself together emotionally—without his physical presence to confuse the issues. Instead of arguing further, she went to retrieve the gun.

Nick took it out of her hand when she returned. With a few quick movements, he checked to see if it was loaded. He flipped the safety off, then back on.

"Do you—" He began to ask her a question, then stopped abruptly. He raised the gun to get a closer look at something.

The changing expression on his face started T.J.'s heart pounding. When he raised his gaze to hers, she knew she was in trouble.

"Where did you get this?"

"I— I bought it at a gun shop near the—"

Nick reached out and clamped one strong hand around her upper arm. In the last twenty-four hours she'd been lulled into a false sense of security by his easy touch and intimate words. Looking into his sudden, dark, suspicious gaze now caused every one of her worst fears to come rushing back.

"Don't lie to me. This weapon has a county serial number. You didn't buy it in any gun shop."

Nick searched T.J.'s turbulent green gaze, and a cold chill ran up his spine. He was glad that he still held the gun. He felt disoriented, as if he'd gone to bed with a soft, beautiful woman and woken with a rattlesnake on his chest. T.J. was lying to him. How many other lies had she told?

"I—" She pulled out of his grasp and moved away.

"Tell me again exactly what kind of story you're doing about the police." He held out the gun. "This is a policeman's weapon. At the very least, it's stolen. How did you get it?"

She stopped to gaze out the front windows into the courtyard. He didn't want to give her enough time to invent a new lie.

"T.J., if you don't tell me the truth, you're going to have to talk to a detective about this weapon. I can't just let it go. Me or a stranger, those are your two choices."

"A stranger would probably be better," T.J. answered in a low voice.

"What? Why?"

"Because, a stranger wouldn't be someone I just made love to."

Nick's anger took a dip. He rubbed his eyes and tried to find his control. "Tell me, T.J. I want to help you. But I can't stand by and watch you break the law."

She turned to face him then. "Neither can I."

"What does that mean?"

"What do you know about a group of bad cops?"

With a long hard look at the woman he knew he was falling for, Nick thought over his response. He'd lied before to get information, but not often. And he didn't like to think lying was necessary with T.J.—regardless of her employment by the newspaper. He answered her truthfully but without giving specifics. "I believe there are as many as five officers on the county force who are involved in illegal activities." He placed the gun on the counter then crossed his arms. "Your turn. What do you know about them?"

T.J. swallowed, visibly nervous. Nick wanted to put her at ease but he needed to know what she'd been up to. He watched and waited.

"That gun isn't stolen. It was . . . given to me as evidence."

"Evidence of what and against whom?"

She didn't answer for several long moments. Nick held himself perfectly still. He could wait as long as it took.

"I want to trust you." Her voice quavered as if she were trying to convince herself. He uncrossed his arms and moved toward her.

"No—" One hand came up to keep him at a distance. "Don't touch me— Just listen."

An unaccountable foreboding ran through Nick. Whatever T.J. intended to tell him was painful. He could see it in her eyes. If it was this difficult, this personal, then he needed to hear it straight without interruption. "Go on," he coaxed. "Trust me enough to let me help you."

Her words came out in a rush. "I have evidence of several crimes committed nearly three years ago. Robbery, extortion and a shooting . . . a murder. All committed by policemen."

Nick couldn't keep his hands off her for another second. His fingers dug into her shoulders to keep them both steady. "What is it? And who gave it to you?"

T.J. didn't seem to hear him. Her eyes were sparkling with unshed tears as she gazed up at him. The pain in her expression made Nick's chest tight.

"Are you one of them, Nick?"

He didn't trust himself to speak. She still thought he was the boogeyman.

"Dammit! Haven't you believed *anything* I've told you?" He shook her once to punctuate his anger, then let her go and put some space between them.

"I want to believe but I—"

"You know, since I was sixteen years old all I ever wanted to be was a cop. I wanted to be one of the good guys, to make a difference. And I did that until..." He stopped, he couldn't tell her about Gina and the kid and what he'd had to do to protect her. He'd given his word to Gina. Besides, T.J.'d never believe him then. One lie was as good as another.

"It nearly killed me when I lost my job, when I was accused of something that was . . . an accident." He turned and pinned her with an examining gaze. "T.J., you know me. You've been with me— I've been inside you, for God's sake. Do you still think I could be a criminal?"

She stared at him, speechless, and Nick felt as if he were facing a loaded gun. Her response could cut him down as quick and as sure as any armor piercing bullet.

T.J. blinked and a cascade of tears spilled over and down her face. "No. I think...you're one of the good guys."

Relieved, Nick ran a hand through his hair and down the back of his neck. His muscles were as tight as a wire. She'd said the right words but she'd looked as though it had broken her heart to do so. He hadn't realized until then how much he needed more than a physical response from her. He needed her approval, her trust. He wanted all of her, heart and mind.

He moved closer and settled her against his chest. He closed his eyes for a moment and drew in the familiar smell of her hair. He'd kill anyone who tried to hurt her. "Come on, hon. Let's sit down. Tell me about it. You don't have to do everything on your own."

T.J. allowed Nick to pull her into his arms because she needed his touch. She needed strength to finish what she'd begun. Because after he knew everything, he'd never feel the same about her. She hadn't realized how much that part of her confession would hurt. She stopped him as he tugged her toward the couch.

"I don't want to sit down. I want to tell you and get it over with." She swallowed against the growing dryness of her throat. "I have a briefcase with tapes and signed statements along with that gun."

"Where did you get it?"

T.J. took a deep breath, intending to blurt out the truth. "I'm—" Staring into his dark, serious gaze, the truth stuck in her throat. *I'm Commissioner Tilton's daughter, Rusty's sister. I'm a woman who has made love with the man who killed her brother.* She wasn't strong enough to see the look on his face when she told him that.

"I got it from...an informant. I can't tell you who."

"If you got it from someone who isn't righteous enough to be a witness then how do you know the evidence is real?"

"It's real." T.J. couldn't tell him any more than that. Besides, all he had to do was play the tapes to know how genuine the accusations and crimes were. Deathbed confessions were hard to dispute and suicide qualified under that heading. She didn't want to be there when Nick heard his friend Mike talk about the crimes. She'd only been able to listen to part of one of the tapes herself before shutting off the machine.

"Show me what you have."

"I was afraid to keep it here." *Because of you.* "It's at Jackson's."

Nick looked surprised. "Jackson? How is he involved in this?"

"He's not involved," T.J. said in a hurry. "He's doing me a favor, that's all. He doesn't even know what's in the briefcase."

"And you think he wouldn't look? Come on." He took her arm. "Let's go get it." As he passed the counter he picked up the gun and slipped it into his jacket pocket.

T.J. allowed herself to be escorted along until they reached Jackson's door. Then she straightened away from Nick's grip and rang the bell.

Jackson opened the door and a flurry of warm air and loud music surrounded them. He either sensed their mood or read the expression on their faces because his neutral, unaffected demeanor changed radically.

"What's up?" He concentrated his attention on T.J.

"I need the briefcase."

Jackson gave Nick an unhurried assessment before he moved back to allow them inside. "Come in."

T.J. self-consciously waved hello to the people inside Jackson's living area. She knew most of her neighbors and tried to look happy and unconcerned for everyone's benefit. A couple of them called out, "Merry Christmas!" T.J. pasted a smile on her face and returned their greetings. Nick stood and frowned like a policeman about to make an arrest.

"This way," Jackson said and led them toward the door to his studio.

Once inside, Jackson flipped on the overhead lights and turned to face them. With the steel door between them and the party, the music faded to a dull beat. T.J. shivered in the cold of the unheated air and from what she was about to do. She was trusting Nick with her life, and possibly with Jackson's. If her judgment about his character had been clouded by her attraction to him, they'd be in serious trouble. T.J. sighed. It was too late to worry about that now. Besides, she was worn out with being responsible for everyone. The time had come to let part of that go, to trust something or someone, for better or worse.

"I want you to give Nick the briefcase," she said to Jackson.

"Are you sure?" he asked before looking at Nick. "Will she be safer then, or in even more danger?"

"Nothing is going to happen to her," Nick answered without elaborating. "I need to see what's in the briefcase so I can decide what to do with it."

T.J. felt a shiver of warning. What did he mean "decide what to do with it"? "You'll take it to the police, right? Someone you can trust."

"I have to see if it's worth pursuing. You can't go after these guys with weak evidence. We only get one shot at them. If they are acquitted, they can't be tried again."

And what if he decides not to pursue it? Like the prosecutor who'd looked into Rusty's death, T.J.'s fear prompted. She shook off the feeling. She trusted Nick.

"Give it to him, Jackson. I can't keep hiding it forever."

Without any further argument, Jackson walked in the direction of his smelting furnace. On one side of the now cool furnace was a neat set of bins holding different lengths of metal and wire. On the far side near the wall was a haphazardly stacked scrap-recycle pile nearly three feet tall. Jackson used a long bar of steel to poke through the pile then lift the top layers. The muscles in his arms bunched against the weight. He motioned for Nick to reach in and retrieve the briefcase.

As soon as Nick's arm had cleared the pile, Jackson let the scrap fall back with a noisy clatter. "Figured I'd hide the trash with the trash," he said, wiping his hands on a rag draped over the furnace safety railing.

"How do you plan to protect T.J. when this information gets out?" he asked Nick.

Nick shifted his gaze from the briefcase to Jackson. "Easy," he answered. "I'm not going to tell anyone she gave it to me." He walked over to a counter near the wall and put the case down. He began to peel off the tape.

"No!" Adrenaline made T.J.'s voice sound louder than she'd intended.

Nick slanted her a puzzled gaze but he stopped working on the tape.

"Not here." She swallowed hard. Panic prompted her to postpone the inevitable for just a bit longer. "Take it and do what you think should be done, but don't involve Jackson. It's bad enough that he hid it for me. The less he sees, the better."

A true reason, but a flimsy one, T.J. decided as she tried to stare the two men down. Jackson was as interested in the contents as Nick but for different reasons. After all, his father had been a cop. And, on top of that, she knew Jackson didn't particularly trust this man who'd bullied his way into her life. What would he say if he knew Nick had killed her brother?

She was the coward. She didn't want to see Nick's face after he knew the whole truth.

Blessedly, he gave in and tucked the case under his arm.

Jackson accompanied Nick and T.J. out of the studio and back to his front door. When Nick stepped outside, T.J. remained inside next to Jackson. She wouldn't, no, couldn't, be there when he went through the contents of the case. The tapes and files would answer many of his questions about the bad cops and about why his friend had committed suicide. But it would also open a host of new questions about her. Questions she wasn't ready to answer.

"You coming?" Nick asked as he held the door open.

"No," she answered. Jackson's silent presence gave her an excuse to skip explanations. "You have what you wanted. My gift to you."

T.J. recognized the war of indecision on Nick's face. He wanted to go through the briefcase, and he wanted her with him.

"I'll be fine here. These are all friends. Go on, do what you have to do." *I've trusted you. It's in your hands now.*

Nick's gaze shifted to Jackson. "You'll make sure she gets back to her place."

Jackson nodded assent.

Nick leaned forward and kissed her lightly. "Stay put, lock your doors. I'll be back or call as soon as I can."

She could only nod.

He still seemed reluctant to leave. Someone called Jackson's name along with a question and it broke the tension. Nick squeezed her hand once then paced off into the darkened courtyard.

"Merry Christmas," T.J. said under her breath as she watched him walk away.

11

NICK WAVED TO to the security guard as he crossed the parking lot of the Coach Works, his mind occupied with mapping out a plan of action. Contrary to his words to T.J., he knew what he carried in the briefcase had to be important. The presence of a traceable weapon announced that fact. He'd waited and watched, and dug around for years searching for something he could use against Lieutenant Echols and Nesmith. Now, he had the distinct feeling that he'd just been presented with the mother lode.

As he walked, his eyes scanned the cars in the well-lit lot, looking for anyone hanging around, any possible source of trouble. If someone was watching T.J., he'd be able to spot them. The lot was crowded with cars, but nothing seemed out of place or sinister. He reached his black Trooper, disabled the alarm, then opened the driver and the rear doors. After wrapping the briefcase in the rain slicker he kept on the back seat, he placed it on the floor, slammed the door and slid into the driver's seat.

He pulled out of the lot with a squeal of tires and headed straight for a twenty-four hour diner he knew. Nothing like hiding in plain sight. He'd open the briefcase and go through it there. Then, if the evidence warranted it, he'd call Internal Affairs and cheerfully interrupt their Christmas plans.

T.J. WAITED FOR fifteen minutes before she decided it was safe to leave Jackson's apartment. Nick had to be long gone.

Jackson caught her opening the door.

"I thought you felt safer in a crowd?"

"I'm not afraid anymore."

He looked unconvinced. When a loud burst of laughter drifted from the living room, he moved to stand between her and the party guests.

"Are you sure? You know I've been trying like hell to help you but that's hard to do when you keep acting brave."

T.J. couldn't stop a sad smile. He'd seen right through her all along. Except now she was telling the truth. She wasn't afraid...well, not of the police. They could do what they would; the evidence and the outcome was out of her hands. Her only fear revolved around Nick; how she felt about him and how it would break her heart to tell him the truth about herself, about her plan to make him pay for her brother's death.

The bottom line was that he'd trusted her, regardless of her lies and her deceptions. He'd stayed and he'd touched her—first through physical attraction, then straight to her heart. She didn't want him to suffer any more than he had, than they all had. And now that her plan for revenge had lost its appeal, she had no sane reason to rationalize being with Nick. She wished she'd given him a better goodbye.

"I'm not being brave. I just need some time alone to think," she said, finally. "I spent the last twenty-four hours with DeSalvo breathing down my neck. I want to go back to my place, put on some soft music, prop my feet up and relax."

Jackson pushed the door wider and held it for her. "Come on then, I'll walk you over."

As T.J. crossed the courtyard with Jackson, she realized that as soon as Nick had gone through the contents of the briefcase, he'd call her. Or, show up like he'd promised. And he'd have more than togetherness on his mind. She just couldn't face his questions tonight.

Jackson waited while she opened the door. He looked so concerned that, impulsively, she rose on her tiptoes and kissed him on the cheek.

"What was that for?" he asked with an unconvincing frown.

"For being a friend."

Jackson stared at her nonplussed, then the corners of his mouth kicked up into a half smile. Like a salute, he tipped his bottle of beer in her direction. He started to turn away, then stopped. "Oh, tell DeSalvo to call me when he gets back here. I want to know how things went."

"I'll tell him," T.J. promised, smiling, lying again. She couldn't tell Nick to call Jackson when he showed up, because she didn't intend to be here.

NICK SETTLED INTO a chair across the table from Edwards and Jessup, fighting the cold, empty feeling in his gut. They'd left the diner and adjourned to Jessup's office in the county building in order to listen to the tapes.

What Nick was about to do ranked in painful duty right up there with attending Mike's funeral. He was about to turn over evidence that his buddy, his best friend, had stepped over the line, had become what Nick had thought they both hated—a criminal.

By the time the Internal Affairs officers had met him at the Metropolitan Diner, Nick had gone through the files and papers in the briefcase. The evidence was well-documented and strong. And all compiled and signed by Officer Mike Tarantino.

Why hadn't he said something? How could he have led this double life without Nick ever suspecting him? Until it was too late to help him? Ultimately, it had cost Mike his future, not to mention Gina and Emma's, and, his own. The bitter taste in Nick's mouth wouldn't go away. If Mike had trusted him enough, they could have faced this mess together. Suicide wasn't the answer—it was a coward's way out.

On Christmas Eve three years ago, not only had Mike destroyed his family, he'd aborted any chance to save his reputation. Nick was about to turn the illusion of Mike's professional ethics over to the police justice system and Mike wouldn't be there to defend himself. With this much evidence, any memory of his buddy as a good cop would evaporate.

Nick stared at a framed certificate for community service on the wall of Jessup's office as the man set up a tape player. He heard the click of the machine being loaded and turned on. Then he heard Mike's voice.

T.J. MADE IT TO her car without anyone seeing her. She couldn't just sit in her loft and wait for Nick to come back. She didn't have the nerve. So, she'd packed a bag and left a note for him. Now, her options were wide-open. He'd told her to leave town. Finding her gone shouldn't come as such a shock. What she needed at this point, was a place to go. It was getting late and there weren't too many public places open. She wanted to drive and think, to decide what to do next.

She made a right turn out of the parking lot then had to stop at the red light at the end of the block. Headlights flashed in her rearview mirror, and her stomach clenched. She looked back. It wasn't a police car and for a moment, T.J. felt relief. As she waited for the light to change she tried to get a look at the two men in the car but the corner was dark and the only illumination came from their own reflected headlights.

When the light changed, T.J. resolved not to take any chances. She turned right without using her blinker. If the car turned behind her, then she'd have to decide what to do if she was being followed.

The car continued on straight. T.J. sighed in relief.
Nick's words came back to her. *Lock your doors and
stay put*. He'd be furious at her for leaving the Coach
Works but he'd be more than furious when he found
out who she really was. T.J. checked to make sure
she'd locked her car doors and drove on. She couldn't
sit and docilely wait for him to question her, wait for
him to call her a liar, or worse, look at her with con-
tempt. At least this way she could put off the inevitable for a few more hours.

She reached the freeway entrance and automatically took the northbound ramp. In the distance, an
elevated sign advertised a Holiday Inn. The safest
thing would be to get a room for the night—a neutral
place to hole up until she was ready to take Nick on.
Merging into the traffic, she decided to think about
that later. For now, she'd just drive.

IT DIDN'T OCCUR TO Nick until two hours into the
meeting with Jessup and Edwards that T.J. must have
known all along that he was Mike's best friend. Had
she planned the whole scenario in order to get a big
story? Had she kept copies of everything she'd given
him to print in the *Atlanta Times Union*? Just like
they'd printed story after story about him when he'd
been fired?

The thought made him feel sick inside. That would
mean she'd used him, from the very beginning. That
she'd baited him and let him think he was taking care
of everything when all the while she was on the case.

Anything to get the big story. He didn't even want to consider it because he'd not only fallen for her scam, he'd fallen for her, period.

He couldn't believe she didn't feel something for him. He remembered her cool reluctance and then her melting hunger. Her response couldn't have been an act. Staring at the evidence of his best friend's betrayal scattered over the table in front of him, Nick swallowed to ease the scratchiness in his throat and the pain in his chest. He'd been fooled before.

"We're going to need to talk to your informant," Jessup said, leaning back in his chair. He seemed very satisfied with the meeting and not in the least put out with having to open his office on Christmas. He and Edwards had waited a long time for this break. "If we're going to use this information in court we have to know where it came from and where it's been for the last few years."

It was time for Nick to finish the task, to put *everything* on the table. But he'd given his word to T.J. and his word still meant something. "You have enough for several warrants. I'll talk to...the informants and see if they'll cooperate further. How soon will this come down?"

Jessup began gathering up the papers and tapes. "We'll start on the warrants tomorrow." He smiled for the first time that night. "These 'upstanding officers' are going to get their Christmas bonus a couple of days late. I can't wait to deliver it in person."

T.J. WAS EXHAUSTED, almost out of gas. The time had come to either fill the gas tank and make good on her note to Nick by leaving town, or rent a room. After getting on the expressway, she'd driven north, back toward her past. She'd discovered her father's house had been painted a different color, the shutters had been changed and the big oak near the driveway had been cut down.

Sitting in her car staring at the place, she'd felt like a stranger to the neighborhood and to herself. The idea that she'd betrayed her family by caring for Nick DeSalvo hung over her like an onerous shadow. What a mess she'd made of everything. She'd lied to Nick— and to Jackson by omission. And she'd lied to herself. She'd fallen in love with the man who'd killed her brother. How could she ever rationalize that? And once Nick found out, how could he ever look at her with anything but disgust and disbelief?

Yet she wanted to see him, to talk to him, to be held in his arms. T.J.'s hands tightened on the wheel. She couldn't run fast enough or far enough to get away from her fear, or from her heart's wish. She had to go back.

T.J. drove right by the Holiday Inn. She wanted to go home, to lock her doors and unplug the phone. She wanted...no, she couldn't have what she really wanted. She couldn't have justice *and* Nick. So she'd settle for a few hours sleep before she had to face him and what she'd done.

Three blocks from the Coach Works, T.J. stopped at a red light near an all-night market. The store was open but nearly deserted. What claimed T.J.'s attention was the police car parked at the edge of the lot near the automatic car wash. She looked away, trying not to seem nervous or guilty. There were very few cars on the road. Most normal people were home sleeping off Christmas dinner.

The light turned green and T.J. drove forward. The police car didn't move, although the officer behind the wheel watched her drive past. Relieved to be ignored, T.J. glanced in the rearview mirror to make sure. Distracted, she didn't see the dark car with no lights that pulled out in front of her until it was too late.

She almost missed him even then, but ended up clipping the rear quarter panel of his ancient Camaro. The driver got out of the car, as T.J. tried to catch her breath. She wasn't hurt, but her heart was pounding so hard she didn't think she could move. And now she would have to deal with the police again.

She rolled down her window halfway as the other driver approached. It didn't dawn on her until he smiled, that he looked familiar. He'd already reached through the window to unlock the door before she put it together. She never forgot a face she'd photographed. And this was the face of the man she'd put on the front page of the *Atlanta Times Union*—after he'd run through a crowd with a car.

NICK PUSHED the intercom buzzer one more time and held it. He knew it might take T.J. a few moments to reach the door but his patience had run out. He rubbed a hand over his face and waited. He felt as if he'd been running on empty for a week but he couldn't stop now. He had to talk to her.

No answer.

Nick stared at the intercom in disbelief. He pushed the buzzer again. Nothing. Worry overshadowed his irritation. The intercom had been working earlier. His first impulse was to find the security guard and make him open the door. Then he remembered he'd left T.J. at Jackson's. Maybe she'd stayed.

He didn't like the way that idea made him feel. He wanted her safe, but with him—not Jackson. He scanned down the list of names until he found the right buzzer.

It took a while for someone to answer. "Yeah?"

"It's Nick DeSalvo. I need to see T.J."

"She's not here. She's— Wait a second." The door lock clicked and Nick pushed through.

Jackson met him in the courtyard.

"She didn't answer the intercom," Nick said and paced past him.

"I walked her home a couple of hours ago. Maybe she went to bed," Jackson said as he followed him over to T.J.'s loft entrance.

"I have to talk to her." Nick rang the bell then knocked loudly on the door. There was no movement or reply from inside. Then he saw the note.

"Nick—took your advice. Leaving town as you suggested. It's better this way. T.J."

"Dammit!" Nick turned to Jackson. "She says she's leaving town. It's after midnight on Christmas Day. Where the hell would she go?"

Jackson balanced his hands on his hips and shook his head. "She went to school in Kentucky. Maybe she has friends there. Her parents are dead. I haven't heard her mention any other family."

"Did you know about this?"

Jackson swore and his hands tightened into fists. "During all the weirdness that's happened in the last week or so, neither one of you thought it was necessary to tell me a friggin' thing." He looked away and sighed, visibly reining in his temper. Then he answered the question. "If I'd known she wanted to leave, I would've gone along to make sure she got there."

If I'd known, I would have stopped her, Nick thought to himself. But she hadn't told him. She still didn't trust him. The same way Mike hadn't trusted him. What had happened in her life to make her think she had to do everything on her own? He had to know in order to make some sense of it—to make it come out right. And to ease the ache inside him. How could she make love with him and not trust him?

He also needed to know a few other things—like where she'd gotten the briefcase of evidence. He intended to get her face-to-face and annoy the answers out of her if he had to. But first he had to find her.

Nick's beeper went off and he felt a stab of apprehension instead of hope. He'd given T.J. his beeper number but for some reason, he didn't think she'd call him so soon after running away. He yanked it off his belt and held it up to the light to see the message. The number wasn't one he recognized. Maybe Edwards or Jessup needed to ask him one more question.

"Can I use your phone?"

There were only two people left at Jackson's apartment. The party seemed to be winding down. Jackson handed Nick a portable phone and walked into the living room to turn the music off.

Nick dialed the number and waited.

"DeSalvo," the man said. No greeting, no question. Nothing to help Nick recognize the man's voice.

"Yeah?"

"Do you know who this is?"

"Why don't you tell me?" He'd lost his patience with games years ago.

"Better yet, do you know who *this* is?" Nick heard the phone being shifted, a muffled sound then a gasp of breath.

"Nick?" The terror in T.J.'s voice made Nick's chest constrict.

12

GOD—NO. Nick felt as though he'd been blindsided by a train. "T.J.? Where—"

"I want to talk to you." The harsh male voice returned. Then the man laughed and Nick suddenly knew who it was.

"Echols. You bastard. She has nothing to do with what's between me and you."

"She's my insurance. We're in a warehouse—3457 Huff Road. Don't make any phone calls. Be here in ten minutes, alone, or your little photographer will wish she was dead."

Jackson stopped Nick on his way out the door. He'd obviously heard Nick's side of the conversation. "I'm going with you."

Nick shook him off. "I have to go alone or they'll hurt her."

"And what do you think they'll do when you get there? Let her go?"

A red haze of fury ran through Nick. With a vicious curse he spun and punched the door causing it to crash against the wall. The pain in his hand gave him something to concentrate on besides his anger. He had to think straight. Everything he cared about depended on it.

After a short span of utter silence, the two neighbors who'd been leftovers from the party appeared in the doorway.

"Party's over," Jackson said unceremoniously. "Catch you later." Mumbling to each other, the two men made a quick exit and disappeared into the darkness of the courtyard.

Jackson stepped in front of Nick again. "We can take my van. You can drop me off before you get there. At least somebody will know where you are."

Nick absently pulled a handkerchief from his pocket and pressed it to his bloody knuckles. "No. They know my Trooper." He sorted through several ideas. There weren't a lot to choose from. But he had to admit—together, they had a better chance of getting T.J. out alive.

"Let's go. I need to think. He shoved the handkerchief back in his pocket and glanced at his watch. We only have eight minutes."

"WHY ARE YOU doing this?" T.J. asked the man who sat staring at her. "I don't even know you."

"Oh, but I know you," Lieutenant Echols said. "You're Commissioner Tilton's daughter."

T.J.'s stomach lurched. "How did you find out?"

"It wasn't very tough. I needed to know why DeSalvo was so interested in you. I made it my business to find out." He leaned back and gave her a smutty smirk. "What's he trying to do? Make you feel better about killing your little brother? Do you talk about it in bed?"

His words left T.J. speechless with outrage. Her immediate instinct was to scratch his eyes out. Her wrists were manacled with tape, but even so, she had to twist her fingers together in her lap to force herself to remain still.

"Doesn't matter," he continued. He left his seat on the edge of a metal desk and walked to the door to peer through the peephole. "You were just what we needed. I've waited a long time for a way to get rid of Nick DeSalvo."

"Get rid of him?" The shocked question was out before she could stop it.

Echols turned to her again. "Yeah, he gave us some trouble when he was on the force. Always so righteous, like he was the sole defender of police integrity. The only good cop on the force. When he got fired I gave a party in celebration." Echols frowned. It was the first time he'd looked angry since she'd been brought into the room. "But, he just won't let it go. He's still nosing around in my business, trying to find evidence against me. And I don't intend to let him stumble onto a way to burn down my career.

"So, thanks to you, the bottom just dropped out of DeSalvo's life expectancy."

"But—"

The thud of the outer door stopped T.J.'s question. *Nick.*

Nick paced through the dark warehouse behind Nesmith with every molecule of his body on alert. He knew there wasn't much of a chance they'd get out of this, but he had to save T.J. or die trying. It was his fault. They'd been after him all along, not T.J. And, the more he'd protected her, the more he'd put her in danger.

He was walking into this alone and unarmed, not a recipe for an auspicious outcome when dealing with a man like Echols. He and Jackson had only come up with a last resort plan. In five minutes, if no one exited the building, Jackson was going to dial 911 on his cell phone and cause a diversion. Nick had given him his weapon and the keys to the Trooper as a way out if the ploy worked. Nick's only goal was to get T.J. to safety before Echols became violent.

Nesmith opened the door and Nick's first sight of T.J. hardened his resolve. Lieutenant Echols stood behind her with his hand possessively on her shoulder. Nick knew he couldn't act too concerned because Echols would take advantage of that.

"Nick . . ." The fearful tone in her voice made him want to charge into the room and kill Echols for ever getting close to her.

"Hello, DeSalvo." Lieutenant Echols sounded like a man who had dealt himself four aces.

"Nick, don't—" T.J. started to warn him, but Echols put his hand over her mouth to quiet her. He watched Nick to see if he might do something about it.

Not yet, the cop in Nick whispered. *Wait for a better chance.*

"Did you pat him down?" Echols asked Nesmith.

Nesmith nodded. "He's clean."

"Hand me a piece of tape."

Nick purposely didn't look into T.J.'s fearful eyes as Echols plastered a wide piece of packing tape over her mouth. But it was all he could do to ignore the panicked sound of her breathing or the muffled word she tried to say. He swallowed and kept his gaze on Echols.

"You don't need her. Let her go," he managed to say through clenched teeth.

"Oh, she's just a little upset at me right now. I'm sure she'll want to stay and see us take care of you. After all, she helped us set this whole thing up." His hard gaze shifted to Nesmith as if they shared a private joke. "You know we tried to take you out at the demonstration," he said. "Then again, on the street. But you just wouldn't cooperate." Echols moved around T.J.'s chair and pinned Nick with a furious gaze. "I told you not to screw around with me. Now you're history."

T.J. made a desperate sound and shifted in her chair.

"Fine, then deal with me. She has nothing to do with any of this," Nick said, still hoping for a way to get T.J. out of here.

Echols seemed to shake off his anger for a moment and he smiled. Nick experienced a sinking feeling. Anything that made the lieutenant smile wouldn't be good.

"Did you actually think she'd forgive you for killing her brother?"

Nick heard T.J. make another anguished sound but he was still trying to make sense of what Echols had said. "What the hell are you talking about?"

Echols stared at him as if he waited for Nick to get the punch line. Then a huge smile broke over his heavy features. "You don't know, do you?"

"Know what?" He couldn't help it, he looked at T.J. Her eyes were glassy with tears. As he watched the moisture spill down her cheeks and over the tape, she shook her head and her sadness was palpable.

"Remember the boy you shot? Tilton, the commissioner's son—the one that got you fired?" Echols paused dramatically, then continued, "Well, I'd like you to meet his sister, Tara Jeanne Tilton—alias T. J. Amberly."

Nick wasn't sure what happened next. He'd intended to stay frosty and in control but suddenly he found himself with his hands around Echols's throat. An earthquake or explosion rocked the building and the lights went out.

13

T.J. ENDED UP on the floor. The force of Nick's lunge had toppled the chair she'd been sitting in. She rolled and scooted backward to get out of the way. The windowless room was in absolute darkness. Someone, she assumed it was Nesmith, stumbled over her and fell. She felt a hand on her ankle and kicked out blindly. A low curse confirmed her aim. Deprived of sight, she concentrated on listening. She heard the metal desk crash against the wall and the sounds of at least two men in a desperate struggle. Then, she heard a gunshot.

A gasp of pain followed, and everyone in the room seemed to pause. Pure terror constricted T.J.'s heart. She brought her hands up, found the edge of the tape on her face and ripped it away.

"Nick!"

No one answered.

Without preamble, the door flew open, rebounded against the wall with a loud bang and the bright beam from a flashlight illuminated the room. There were three uniformed policemen with guns drawn positioned in the doorway.

"Everybody, freeze!"

T.J. searched for Nick. He had Echols pinned with his arm twisted behind him, the lieutenant's face against the wall. She could see blood but couldn't tell who it belonged to. Nick had a gun in his hand. He raised it, gingerly, to show the police then placed it on the desk. Nesmith didn't move from his position on the floor.

"I said put the weapon down!" the officer ordered.

With every weapon aimed in his direction, Nesmith seemed to think better of putting up a fight. He put his gun down on the floor and pushed it away.

The police entered the room, followed by Jackson. Chaos reigned for a few minutes as everyone began talking at once. Jackson pulled T.J. to her feet and stripped the tape from her wrists. He looked murderous but didn't say a word. T.J. leaned around him to find Nick. There seemed to be more blood on Echols than on him and when one of the newly arrived officers forced Echols to sit down while he called for an ambulance she knew that Nick must be all right.

But he wouldn't look at her.

"Are you hurt?" Jackson asked after releasing her hands. "Did they do anything to you?"

"No, I'm okay." In truth they hadn't hurt her, physically. Yet, as she watched Nick talk to the uniformed officers and studiously ignore her, she knew Echols's announcement of the truth had managed to wound them both. Her knees suddenly felt like jelly. "I think I need to sit down."

Jackson retrieved the overturned chair and placed it near her. T.J. sat stoically, fighting back tears until one of the officers came over to take her statement.

Forty minutes later, T.J. was told that she could go home. She still hadn't spoken to Nick directly but she accepted Jackson's offer to take her back to the Coach Works. She knew she'd never make it there on her own and she couldn't stay in the same room with Nick and be ignored any longer. It hurt too much.

As Jackson escorted her from the room, she paused at the door to look back one last time. She had the terrible feeling that she might never see Nick again. His eyes met hers directly for the first time since he'd learned who she was. What she saw in his gaze chilled her heart. Nothing. He stared at her as if she were a stranger, an anonymous victim. She turned away and stumbled along with Jackson holding her arm.

They had to make their way around the wreckage in the outer part of the warehouse. A vehicle had crashed through the metal door of the loading dock and now stood stranded in the center of the room amid the rubble.

"I hope DeSalvo has good insurance," Jackson said as he helped her through the gaping hole where the door used to be.

T.J. looked a little closer and realized the vehicle was Nick's Trooper. "Wh-what happened?"

"I needed a way to cause a diversion and get into the building." He shrugged. "And DeSalvo left me his keys."

T.J. would have laughed if she'd had any energy left in her body. But she was too tired and too heartsick. It was all over. Including her relationship with Nick.

They passed three police cars and the ambulance. T.J. saw the man who'd kidnapped her, the man she'd photographed at the demonstration, handcuffed and locked inside the back of one patrol car. They reached her car and Jackson settled her in the passenger side before sliding in to drive. As he put the car in Reverse to turn around, T.J. couldn't resist looking back toward the warehouse. She saw Nick, lit by the flashing blue light of police emergency flashers, standing just outside the door.

A wild ray of hope brightened in her heart. Maybe he wouldn't let her go without a word after all. Maybe he'd come out to stop her. But he didn't speak or raise a hand. He simply watched as Jackson drove out of the lot.

SITTING ON THE BALCONY of her loft in the afternoon sunlight, T.J. sighed and stared blindly out at the horizon. Nick hadn't come for her. Two nights and three days had passed since she'd last seen him. Her life was in perfect order again, business as usual, except for her continuing conversations with the two officers from Internal Affairs, and the prospect of having to testify in court.

She remembered her wish to see Nick DeSalvo in court and how that wish had changed. It looked like the only place she'd ever see Nick again would be

when she testified against Lieutenant Echols and
Nesmith, explaining the connection between her father and Nick's friend Mike Tarantino.

She recognized the hollow feeling of loneliness.
Nick must have believed that she'd set him up. Or
worse, he'd been disgusted by the thought that she'd
given herself to the man who'd killed her brother. And
he hadn't been interested in explanations.

He'd disappeared out of her life as if he'd died on
Christmas night. Without a "goodbye" or "go away,"
she was on her own again. She'd accomplished part
of what she'd wanted, but she'd fallen in love with the
wrong man in the process.

She'd never find out what really happened the night
Rusty died. Not now. She knew one thing, however.
Nick wasn't one of the dirty cops and he hadn't killed
Rusty to protect them. The fact remained, however,
he'd held the gun that killed her brother. And she
loved him just the same.

She wished she could cry and get it over with, but
her eyes were dry and uncooperative. Some part of
her knew that she might never get over Nick. She'd let
him go because she had to, because the truth would
always stand between them. The truth and her lies,
tied together in a tangled package that had exploded
on Christmas night.

The doorbell sounded downstairs. Pushing up from
her seat on the cool metal floor of her balcony she gave
the skyline one last glance. She remembered as a child,
wishing that she could fly. As she stared at the tall

buildings in the distance she realized that even knowing how to fly wouldn't make her happy now. She'd never be able to fly fast enough or far enough to escape her memories, or her broken heart.

By the time she made it downstairs to the door, there was no one there. She opened it and glanced out. Tyler, playing the role of deliveryman, had moved on to the loft next to hers. Seeing her, he waved and walked over to hand her an envelope. Her name was printed on the front in beautiful strokes of calligraphy.

"Hey Cinderella, here's your invitation to the ball New Year's Eve," he said.

"Ball?"

"Yes, and you'll need a dance partner. Bring a date," he ordered. "Glass slippers are optional."

Without wanting to argue or explain why she wouldn't be there, T.J. produced an agreeable smile, waved goodbye and went back inside. She dropped the envelope on the counter and picked up the phone. She'd call her boss at the paper. Maybe she could beg an assignment out of him. There must be something newsworthy going on in this town. Anything to keep her too busy to think.

MUCH LATER that night, T.J. awoke with a start. For several confused seconds she lay in the dark, feeling her heart pound. Something was wrong. Had a dream frightened her awake? She didn't remember any fleeting images or lingering night terrors. It *had* taken her a long time to go to sleep, however, and to wake up for no good reason annoyed her.

She'd spent most of the evening at a charity event given by a local political figure, shooting pictures of couples dancing and eating and pledging their money for a worthy cause. That had been fine with T.J. She knew her job and when she worked, she didn't need a dance partner.

She fluffed her pillow and closed her eyes, determined to doze off again. Sleep was her one escape, the only time she didn't miss Nick, the only time she didn't wonder about what might have happened between them if she'd told him the truth from the beginning.

Then she heard the noise. It came from outside the trapdoor to her balcony. T.J.'s heartbeat took another leap and she sat up. What should she do? She no longer had the gun—Nick had taken it. She glanced around her bed for another kind of weapon but all she found useful was the phone. She quietly scooted to the edge of the bed and with shaking hands picked up the receiver. Dialing 911 would be easy in the dark. She just had to wait quietly.

She had pushed the nine when someone knocked on the window as if they'd come to her front door. Why would a thief or a murderer knock first? She pulled the receiver away from her ear and listened. The knock came again, a bit louder. Then she heard a voice.

"T.J.?"

Her heart gave a lurch and she felt as though she were falling through space. Could her mind be fooling her? "Nick?"

"T.J., let me in. I have to talk to you."

T.J. slowly replaced the phone and forced herself to stand on unstable legs. She started for the window but stopped and spun around looking for her robe. She couldn't greet him in a T-shirt and panties. God knew what he'd come to tell her. She switched on the light by her bed, found the robe, hurriedly pulled it on and stepped up the stairs. She levered open the catch and pushed the window open slightly.

Her first glimpse of him was of one large hand catching the edge of the window and pulling it outward. She realized she would recognize him even if she only saw that much. That hand was also the symbol of what stood between them—Rusty's blood.

She looked into his eyes. He hesitated, filling the space, blocking the night sky behind him as cold air flowed into the room.

"You scared me! Why didn't you call or use the intercom?" T.J. said in the effort to rationalize her wildly beating heart and trembling hands.

"I'm sorry. I needed to talk to you and I wasn't sure you'd let me in." He slipped his hands into the pockets of his jacket. "May I come in?"

His solemn face warned her that he didn't have anything good to say. Too tongue-tied to answer, T.J. could only nod. She pulled her gaze from the welcome sight of him and backed down the stairs.

Well, you're here, get it over with, Nick's conscience whispered. He stepped through the door and pulled it shut behind him. He watched T.J. move toward the bed as if she intended to sit but in the last second she seemed to think better of it and turned to face him. He couldn't blame her. He didn't want to even glance at her bed. He didn't want to remember everything about the steamy night he'd spent in her arms, in her body. Instead of stepping downward and into the room, he sat on the second step from the top, a safe distance from T.J.

"How have you been?" he asked to begin the conversation, to get his mind off what he wanted, who he wanted. She looked thinner and sadder than he remembered, and it took every bit of his willpower not to close the distance between them and drag her into his arms. Bitter pain rose inside him. She wouldn't want that. Of all the cops on duty the night her brother had run, why did he and Gina have to catch him?

"I'm okay," she answered in a low voice, but her expression said something different.

"I've—" *missed you.* He had to swallow the words he wanted to say, the words she wouldn't want to hear. "I . . . came to apologize."

"For what? Saving my life?"

Nick had no answer for that question. He couldn't take credit for something that was his fault to begin with. Echols had been after him all along—not T.J. Nick had put her in danger by pushing his way into her life. He couldn't go into why he'd had to save her or die trying. "No. I want to talk to you about your brother."

"Oh…" The air seemed to go out of her. She slowly sank down to sit on the bed and folded her hands in her lap. The urge to touch her made him shift positions on the stair. He'd known talking to her about the past would be difficult, but he hadn't realized just how difficult. He'd face Echols and a gun ten nights in a row rather than say the words he knew he had to say.

He wanted to tell her the truth, that he hadn't killed her brother. Then, maybe someday she'd forgive him or at least not hate him. But he couldn't tell her about Gina. He'd given his word, he'd sworn under oath. He wasn't going to be the next man after Mike to let Gina down.

And how could confessing to a lie make T.J. love him? There had already been too many lies between them. He ran a hand down his face and mustered his prepared speech.

"It was an accident. I never meant for him to be hurt." T.J. sat watching him with somber eyes. Without making a conscious decision, Nick pushed to his feet and stepped down the stairs. He forced himself to stop a few feet in front of her. "He was running and scared . . . he had a gun."

He heard T.J. take a swift breath as her eyes filled with tears. *Go on, finish it,* his mind ordered. "We— I tried to talk him into putting it down but . . ." He couldn't tell her about seeing that young face…those shaking hands holding a gun pressed to his head. He slipped his hands into his pockets again because if he didn't, he'd grab her to hold her steady, to hold them both steady as he said the words. "We struggled for the gun, and it went off."

She made a sound like a sob and looked down. Nick squatted in front of her to see her face. "I'm so sorry," he said and placed one hand over hers. The contact set off a wave of longing inside him. He'd wanted to see her, to touch her for days and hadn't been able to face her.

T.J. didn't look at him. One of her tears splashed on his knuckles but he couldn't pull his hand away. Even when he remembered that she might not want him to touch her—ever.

"Why didn't you tell me who you are?" he asked. "How could you let me—" *Touch you? Was it just to get a story?* He couldn't finish the accusation out loud. He was afraid she'd withdraw and he needed to know why she'd gotten involved with him. He didn't believe she'd helped Echols, but she must have had her own reasons. And he wasn't leaving until he heard them.

"I couldn't tell you," she answered in a small, tired voice. She met his gaze then. "At first I was angry and afraid. I wanted to hurt you. I thought you had killed Rusty to keep my father from giving evidence about your friends."

A shock wave went through Nick. He was stunned. She'd thought he was a murderer and yet had stood up to him, toe-to-toe. No matter how brave he'd thought she was in the past, he knew now he'd underestimated her courage.

"I wanted you to pay for what you'd done."

Nick remembered all the times he'd seen distrust in her eyes when he'd been doing his best to be trustworthy. He lowered his gaze to their hands.

"How could you stand to let me touch you?" He started to pull away, but she gripped his hand and held on.

"Because my body trusted you. My heart trusted you. I found out I was both wrong and right. And even though you . . . hurt Rusty, you're not a killer. I know that now." She swallowed hard. "And I didn't set you up," she added.

"I knew you didn't." Nick brushed his fingers along her cheekbone, then curled them around her neck before he drew in a steadying breath. "And I know you don't want to hear this, but I've fallen in love with you." She started to speak but he stopped her. "I'm not asking for anything—except maybe forgiveness. I can't change the past but you have to know I would if I could. I'd do anything to make it different."

In the next few seconds, T.J.'s arms went around his neck. She pushed her face against his throat and he could feel her tears on his skin, her ragged breath against his chest. He slowly raised her to her feet and held on while she cried. It was the least he could do before he walked out of her life forever.

Nick's words echoed in T.J.'s heart. *I can't change the past.* Neither of them could change it. But could they change the future? Could they ever find a way past the guilt and the pain? T.J. didn't know, but she knew she wasn't ready to let Nick go. Not until they'd tried.

She sucked in a deep breath, swallowed back her tears, and raised her chin until her lips brushed his throat, slightly below his jaw. She wet his skin with her tongue then kissed the same spot. "Nick?" she whispered against his neck.

The pressure of his arms and hands shifted from comforting to tense. She felt him swallow before he answered. "Yeah?"

She brought one hand upward along his chest and around his neck to push her fingers into his hair. She wanted him to kiss her, to love her, to stay with her just a little longer until she could think of a way to hold on to what they both wanted—to be together. Her guilt wouldn't let her say what her heart felt, so she'd show him with her body.

"Kiss me . . . please."

A tremor ran through his arms. He gently kissed her temple, her cheekbone. "T.J. . . . ." He said her name with sadness, reluctance. "I can't. That's not why I came here tonight. If I kiss you, we'll end up . . . I won't have you look at me tomorrow with regret. I need all of you, not just . . . this." His hands tightened on her back momentarily, then loosened as if to let her go.

T.J. held on. "I need all of you, too," she confessed looking into his eyes. "I don't know how to make us work...how to love you without thinking of the past, but I want to try. At least now we both know the truth."

He looked so uncomfortable for a moment, T.J. thought he didn't want her. That he intended to say goodbye forever. Then his gaze shifted downward to her mouth and he groaned like a man in pain.

He kissed her, slow and deep and long, as if he couldn't get enough of her mouth or her taste. A familiar languorous warmth simmered through T.J.'s body. Her arms and legs felt heavy, her senses drugged. His hands slid inside her robe and bunched her T-shirt upward to slip beneath.

Her hands fumbled with his jacket, pushing it off his shoulders until he had to release her to get out of it. She shrugged out of her robe and went to work on the buttons of his shirt as his mouth covered hers once more, stroking, sucking.

He had to finish the last two buttons because T.J.'s fingers had found better things to do, like exploring the hard, warm expanse of his chest. Even the familiar rough shape of the scar below his collarbone.

Nick felt T.J.'s hand brush the scar from the bullet her brother had fired and knew he'd sold his soul. She'd said they both knew the truth but there was one more lie between them. He didn't care, couldn't muster up enough fear to worry. She hadn't said she loved him, precisely. But, she'd said she wanted to try. He couldn't pass up the chance. If she still wanted him after all the things she thought he'd done, then she must love him. Only love could overcome those odds.

And he was crazy enough about her to overlook anything at this point. He pressed upward underneath the soft material of her shirt until her breasts filled his palms. T.J. moaned and Nick lost the ability to think of anything beyond that sweet sound and the way it turned him inside out.

14

IT WAS SORT OF like walking on eggshells, Nick decided as he removed his suit jacket from the garment hook and slammed the door of his rental car. He and T.J. They'd spent the last few days and nights getting to know each other again, testing the depth and width of their feelings for each other. And now it was New Year's Eve and they were going public.

A new beginning. Tonight at the Coach Works New Year's Eve party, it would be the first time they'd presented themselves as a couple publicly. And although Nick wasn't wild about the whole idea of partying to bring in the New Year, he wouldn't miss this one. He liked the idea of being T.J.'s date and he intended to make sure she enjoyed herself instead of thinking too much.

He waved to the security guard then punched in the resident's code to open the door. When it clicked and opened, he smiled to himself. At least he wouldn't have to climb the wall again to get to the woman he loved. He had her number, so to speak.

His beeper went off.

Switching his keys and his jacket to one hand, he looked at the number on the message. Gina. Damn. He hoped nothing was wrong. He'd spent most of the day before with her as she learned the full extent of Mike's involvement in Echols and Nesmith's criminal activities. He'd also told her about him and T.J. About how much he wanted to work things out between them, to have a life together. At the time, she'd told him she was happy for him. But this call worried him. Had something else bad happened?

He reached T.J.'s door and rang the bell. When she opened it, he stopped in his tracks. She was wearing a short little black dress that shimmered like wet velvet in the light. She'd pinned most of her long blond hair up and back, except for a few enticing loose strands.

"You look terrific," he said in total awe. He'd seen her naked, yet something about the way the fabric of the dress clung to her hips and breasts, the way the sheer stockings she wore gave a subtle sheen to her long legs made his mouth go dry. He instantly started planning exactly how he would get her out of that dress.

"Thank you," she replied with a mysterious smile.

He hung his jacket on the back of the doorknob, kissed her lightly and breathed in the fragrance of her perfume. His mind, however, was still hung up on her legs. "Are those stockings or panty hose?" he asked, his lips close to her ear.

"Stockings."

He casually ran one hand along the back of her thigh, skimming upward under the edge of the dress until he reached bare skin. He stroked her upper thigh in fascination then nipped her ear. "And how long do we have to stay at this party?"

T.J. dipped her head toward him, bringing her mouth closer. "At least until midnight." Her voice poured through his senses like warm honey. They both knew the game and wanted to play. It made Nick feel like laughing out loud.

"Damn. I have the feeling the first time I see you sit down in this dress I'm going to have a heart attack." He removed his hand with a great show of reluctance, straightened the hemline of the dress and kissed her again briefly. He set her away from him as if that would keep her safe and in her party clothes. Then he gave her his best lecherous smile. "Both of us will have to stand up all night. So, if you get a headache or your feet hurt and you need to come home early, let me know."

T.J. laughed and Nick experienced something he hadn't felt in a long, long time. Hope. Maybe they could make it after all.

The phone rang. T.J. was still smiling at him when she picked it up.

"Hello?

"Oh, hi Gina." Her smile faltered slightly and Nick walked toward her. "Yes, we're going to a party here at the Coach Works." She listened for another moment without speaking.

Nick got nervous. He should have called Gina right away, but his mind had turned to jelly the moment he'd seen T.J.'s legs. He held out his hand for the phone, but T.J. didn't give it up.

"Well, why don't you stop by here after you get off?" T.J.'s invitation sounded genuine if not effusive. He hoped she didn't feel obligated to invite Gina to the party and wondered why Gina hadn't asked for him.

"I understand. Yes, I'm sure Tyler won't care. He loves big parties. Please come by. Okay. Do you want to speak to Nick?"

Nick put his hand over T.J.'s on the receiver but she still didn't release it. "All right, I'll tell him. See you later." T.J. pulled the phone away and hung it up.

"Gina said, don't bother to call her back. She just wanted to know if we had plans for tonight."

"Why?"

"She didn't say why. You don't mind that I invited her, do you?"

Nick thought about it for a moment. The entire call had sounded like some kind of female conspiracy. Then he mentally shrugged off his natural suspicion. Surely the two women closest to him wouldn't plan something to make him worry. And, after all, he wanted them to be friends. "No, I don't mind as long as you don't."

"I don't."

T.J. kissed him and straightened his tie. It was such an affectionate, *wifely* thing to do that Nick knew then and there he would ask her to marry him. Maybe even tonight at midnight—right before he went to work on whatever feminine magic she'd enlisted to hold up her stockings.

"Are you ready to make our appearance?" she asked.

He stared into the warm depths of her green eyes and smiled. "Let's do it."

THE NOVA GALLERY was the larger of the two spacious rooms that comprised the commercial space at the heart of the Coach Works. As she and Nick strolled through the entrance, they paused to take in the full effect. T.J. decided that Tyler had outdone himself. The theme for the party was stardust. From twinkling lights in the greenery to spirals of sparkling silver star garland hanging from the ceiling, the large room looked like a glitter factory that had exploded.

"Welcome," Tyler said, meeting them at the door like the mâitre d'. He looked spectacular in his custom fitted tuxedo. Dapper enough to attend a ball at the governor's mansion, except for the headgear: two Mylar stars bobbed crazily from wires attached to a headband. Knowing Tyler, he'd probably invited the governor to tonight's party.

"Tyler? You remember Nick?"

"Yes." Tyler extended his hand to Nick in greeting.

"This place looks wonderful," T.J. said. "And you do, too." She twanged the wire holding one of the stars and set them in motion, then smiled at Nick. "You need one of these."

"Oh, no you don't. You can't have my stars," Tyler said, backing out of range. "There are plenty of hats and toys over by the punch bowl."

T.J. looked in the direction Tyler indicated and saw Jackson across the room talking to one of their neighbors. She almost didn't recognize him. Dressed in a pair of black jeans that fit as if he'd been born in them and a black pullover sweater, his longish hair brushed back out of his face, he looked . . . nearly as gorgeous as Nick. She realized she'd never seen him in anything other than threadbare jeans or leather—the typical guy next door. And she couldn't believe he'd attended the party alone. Her curiosity piqued by the change, she drew Nick in that direction.

"You totaled my Trooper," Nick said in greeting as he extended his hand to Jackson.

"You should be more careful who you leave it with." Jackson released Nick's hand then crossed his arms and smirked. "If you're gonna whine about it, I'll buy the wreck from you and use the pieces in the next bridge I build."

"I'll give you the number of my insurance agent," Nick offered. "He's the one who's whining."

T.J. glanced around the immediate area. "Where's Rita?"

"She's in New York . . . with her fiancé, I would imagine," Jackson said, in an unconcerned tone. He might just as well have been talking about the weather.

"But—" T.J. began.

Jackson raised a hand to stop her. "Don't get all concerned about it. Her New Year's resolution was to get married. Mine wasn't. We're still friends."

At that moment, the volume of the music increased. Tyler, along with his significant other, Steve, started making their way around the room coaxing other couples to dance. By the time they reached T.J., Nick and Jackson, several people were moving out onto the dance floor.

"Come on, you two," Tyler said to Nick and T.J. Then he glanced at Jackson and frowned. "You were supposed to bring a date," he said unceremoniously.

"Sorry, I'm fresh out of women at the moment." Jackson's mouth quirked with a sardonic smile. "You want me to dance with Steve?"

Tyler rolled his eyes. "Steve is *my* date," Tyler said as if Jackson had suffered brain damage from the punch. "You can just stand here alone and spoil the symmetry." With a huff of exasperation, Tyler moved along to the next group of guests.

"You are incorrigible," T.J. said to Jackson as Nick entwined his fingers with hers.

"Dance with me," Nick said as he pulled her toward the center of the room.

In the next two hours the party cranked up. Somewhere around eleven, as T.J. listened to Nick discuss gun control with one of her neighbors over the beat of an oldie rock-and-roll tune, she glanced up and saw Gina at the entrance to the gallery. Still dressed in her police uniform but without her gun and radio, she seemed reluctant to come in. Not wanting to interrupt Nick, T.J. squeezed his arm and slipped away. Gina had asked to speak to her alone when she'd called and T.J. wanted to know why.

Jackson caught her halfway to the entrance. "What's this with the police? Are you in trouble again?"

"Not to worry, she's a friend." She patted his arm.

"She doesn't look very friendly."

T.J. raised one hand and waved to get Gina's attention. "She doesn't know anyone here except Nick and me. Be nice." Gina hesitantly returned the greeting and moved in their direction.

"Hi, Gina," T.J. said as the woman approached.

"Hi." Gina scanned the room for a moment. "This is some party."

"Yeah, Tyler loves to celebrate. Oh, Gina Tarantino, this is Jackson Gray, one of my neighbors."

Gina looked up at Jackson and offered him her hand in a businesslike manner. T.J. hadn't realized until that moment how tiny Gina was. Dressed in her uniform with her dark hair pulled back in a clip, she gave a formidable impression, but she appeared fragile standing next to Jackson.

"Nice to meet you," Gina said to Jackson and released his hand. Her gaze scanned the room again. She looked a little nervous. She turned her attention to T.J. "I'd like to talk to you . . . without Nick around."

"Okay, let's walk over to my place. Jackson? If Nick starts looking for me, keep him occupied, okay?"

Jackson nodded. "You got it. You'll be back, right?"

"Right," T.J. answered and moved with Gina toward the door.

They walked through the open entryway, then into the courtyard. The night was clear and cold and absolutely still. Gina paused by a bench situated under a tree. The waning moon painted shadow patterns on the ground at their feet.

"It's really nice here," Gina said taking a deep breath.

"Yeah. I like it a lot. My loft is right over there."

T.J. led Gina to the door and opened it. When they were inside, Gina spent a few seconds collecting herself and T.J.'s stomach did a fluttery roll. She began to worry.

"First I want you to know how happy I am that you and Nick...are together," Gina began. "I can't imagine what you must have been through in these last weeks."

"What did you want to talk to me about?" T.J. asked unable to wait any longer. She'd just found her equilibrium again after the kidnapping, and her confrontation with Nick about Rusty. The thought of facing more bad news made her queasy.

"I want to tell you about the night your brother died."

NICK HAD BEEN entertained, or closer to the mark, *detained* by Jackson for almost thirty minutes when he saw Gina walk into the room. Where the hell was

T.J.? He put down the drink he'd been holding and met her with Jackson walking silently behind him.

"What's going on? Where's T.J.?" he asked without even a hello. He didn't want to deal with any weirdness tonight—not tonight.

Gina looked as though she'd been crying. She gave him a tremulous smile then rose on her tiptoes and kissed him on the cheek. "Happy New Year, Nick."

"Yeah, hon. Same to you. Where's—"

"She's over at her place," Gina said. "She said to tell you she has a pounding headache."

"What? She was fine a little while—"

"I think you should go check on her," Gina said and patted his arm.

Nick left Gina standing with Jackson. He deserted the party, cut across the grass of the courtyard and didn't pause to knock on T.J.'s door. He found her standing in the middle of the living room with her hands braced on her hips. Before he could open his mouth she beat him to it.

"I could kill you," she said, and then threw her arms around him.

He held on to her, waiting for an explanation. Death didn't seem such a high price to pay as long as he had T.J. in his arms.

"What did I do?" he asked pulling her closer.

She squirmed back away from him and looked into his eyes. "Gina told me the truth. You didn't shoot Rusty, he shot you." She touched his jaw with her fingers and Nick felt his heart slow to a hard painful beat. "Why didn't you tell me?"

"I couldn't— I gave my word and I— Damn!" He tried to pull away from her, to give them both some space so he could explain but she wouldn't let him go. He sighed. "I didn't want any more lies between us. But I also wanted you—any way I could have you."

"You've got me." She kissed him lightly on the lips. Her eyes sparkled with unshed tears. "I loved you even though I thought you'd hurt my brother. I love you even more now." She brought her smooth cool hands up to bracket his jaw. "Gina said she wants to make a new beginning, and she wanted us to have one, too."

At that moment, a burst of firecrackers went off in the courtyard and several voices shouted, "Happy New Year!"

Nick looked at the woman he loved and said the words he'd been planning all night. "Let's make it a real beginning. Marry me."

She met his gaze without blinking. "I will," she said solemnly as if they were standing in front of a priest.

Then he kissed her. After several long moments, T.J. pulled back and drew in a deep breath. "Should we go out and make the announcement?"

"Later— Tomorrow," he mumbled against her neck as his hands slid down along the hem of her dress. "You've got a headache and I have to investigate these stockings." He found bare skin and followed it to the edge of her panties.

"Nick?" Her breathless voice sent a sharp thrill of pleasure through him.

"Hmmm?" He kissed then sucked the spot just under her ear.

"Happy New Year," she managed to say.

He laughed and drew in a breath near her ear. "You want to see happy and new? You ain't seen nothin' yet."

Epilogue

"HAPPY NEW YEAR!"

Gina watched the couples around her at the party embrace and kiss. It would be a *new* year, she decided. She'd make it so. She'd sacrificed her present for the past long enough.

She turned to the tall, striking man standing near her, a stranger really except that she knew his name—Jackson Gray—and raised her glass of champagne for a toast.

"Happy New Year," she said. He clinked his glass to hers and followed her action of taking a ceremonial sip. Then he pulled the glass from her hand and set both his and hers on a nearby table.

"I guess this will be a new year for me." His fingers slipped upward along the sleeves of her uniform. "I've never kissed a cop before," he said as he bent toward her.

Then his mouth touched hers.

* * * * *

*Be sure to watch for Gina and Jackson's
story in #618, NEW YEAR'S KNIGHT,
available in January 1997.*

INSTANT WIN 4229 SWEEPSTAKES
OFFICIAL RULES

1. NO PURCHASE NECESSARY. YOU ARE DEFINITELY A WINNER. For eligibility, play your instant win ticket and claim your prize as per instructions contained thereon. If your "Instant Win" ticket is missing or you wish another, send a self-addressed, stamped envelope (WA residents need not affix return postage) to: Instant Win 4229 Ticket, P.O. Box 9045, Buffalo, NY 14269-9045 in the U.S., and in Canada, P.O. Box 609, Fort Erie, Ontario, L2A 5X3. Only one (1) "Instant Win" ticket will be sent per outer mailing envelope. Requests received after 12/30/96 will not be honored.

2. Prize claims received after 1/15/97 will be deemed ineligible and will not be fulfilled. The exact prize value of each Instant Win ticket will be determined by comparing returned tickets with a prize value distribution list that has been preselected at random by computer. Prizes are valued in U.S. currency. For each one million, or part thereof, tickets distributed, the following prizes will be made available: 1 at $2,500 cash; 1 at $1,000 cash; 3 at $250 cash each; 5 at $50 cash each; 10 at $25 cash each; 1,000 at $1 cash each; and the balance at 50¢ cash each. Unclaimed prizes will not be awarded.

3. Winner claims are subject to verification by D. L. Blair, Inc., an independent judging organization whose decisions on all matters relating to this sweepstakes are final. Any returned tickets that are mutilated, tampered with, illegible or contain printing or other errors will be deemed automatically void. No responsibility is assumed for lost, late, nondelivered or misdirected mail. Taxes are the sole responsibility of winners. Limit: One (1) prize to a family, household or organization.

4. Offer open only to residents of the U.S. and Canada, 18 years of age or older, except employees of Harlequin Enterprises Limited, D. L. Blair, Inc., their agents and members of their immediate families. All federal, state, provincial, municipal and local laws apply. Offer void in Puerto Rico, the province of Quebec and wherever prohibited by law. All winners will receive their prize by mail. Taxes and/or duties are the sole responsibility of the winners. No substitution for prizes permitted. Major prize winners may be asked to sign and return an Affidavit of Eligibility within 30 days of notification. Noncompliance within this time or return of affidavit as undeliverable may result in disqualification, and prize may never be awarded. By acceptance of a prize, winners consent to the use of their names, photographs or other likeness for purposes of advertising, trade and promotion on behalf of Harlequin Enterprises Limited, without further compensation, unless prohibited by law. In order to win a prize, residents of Canada will be required to correctly answer a time-limited arithmetical skill-testing question to be administered by mail.

5. For a list of major prize winners (available after 2/14/97), send a self-addressed, stamped envelope to: "Instant Win 4229 Sweepstakes" Major Prize Winners, P.O. Box 4200, Blair, NE 68009-4200, U.S.A.

MILLION DOLLAR SWEEPSTAKES
OFFICIAL RULES
NO PURCHASE NECESSARY TO ENTER

1. To enter, follow the directions published. Method of entry may vary. For eligibility, entries must be received no later than March 31, 1998. No liability is assumed for printing errors, lost, late, non-delivered or misdirected entries.
   To determine winners, the sweepstakes numbers assigned to submitted entries will be compared against a list of randomly, preselected prize winning numbers. In the event all prizes are not claimed via the return of prize winning numbers, random drawings will be held from among all other entries received to award unclaimed prizes.

2. Prize winners will be determined no later than June 30, 1998. Selection of winning numbers and random drawings are under the supervision of D. L. Blair, Inc., an independent judging organization whose decisions are final. Limit: one prize to a family or organization. No substitution will be made for any prize, except as offered. Taxes and duties on all prizes are the sole responsibility of winners. Winners will be notified by mail. Odds of winning are determined by the number of eligible entries distributed and received.

3. Sweepstakes open to residents of the U.S. (except Puerto Rico), Canada and Europe who are 18 years of age or older, except employees and immediate family members of Torstar Corp., D. L. Blair, Inc., their affiliates, subsidiaries, and all other agencies, entities, and persons connected with the use, marketing or conduct of this sweepstakes. All applicable laws and regulations apply. Sweepstakes offer void wherever prohibited by law. Any litigation within the province of Quebec respecting the conduct and awarding of a prize in this sweepstakes must be submitted to the Régie des alcools, des courses et des jeux. In order to win a prize, residents of Canada will be required to correctly answer a time-limited arithmetical skill-testing question to be administered by mail.

4. Winners of major prizes (Grand through Fourth) will be obligated to sign and return an Affidavit of Eligibility and Release of Liability within 30 days of notification. In the event of non-compliance within this time period or if a prize is returned as undeliverable, D. L. Blair, Inc. may at its sole discretion, award that prize to an alternate winner. By acceptance of their prize, winners consent to use of their names, photographs or other likeness for purposes of advertising, trade and promotion on behalf of Torstar Corp., its affiliates and subsidiaries, without further compensation unless prohibited by law. Torstar Corp. and D. L. Blair, Inc., their affiliates and subsidiaries are not responsible for errors in printing of sweepstakes and prize winning numbers. In the event a duplication of a prize winning number occurs, a random drawing will be held from among all entries received with that prize winning number to award that prize.

5. This sweepstakes is presented by Torstar Corp., its subsidiaries and affiliates in conjunction with book, merchandise and/or product offerings. The number of prizes to be awarded and their value are as follows: Grand Prize — $1,000,000 (payable at $33,333.33 a year for 30 years); First Prize — $50,000; Second Prize — $10,000; Third Prize — $5,000; 3 Fourth Prizes — $1,000 each; 10 Fifth Prizes — $250 each; 1,000 Sixth Prizes — $10 each. Values of all prizes are in U.S. currency. Prizes in each level will be presented in different creative executions, including various currencies, vehicles, merchandise and travel. Any presentation of a prize level in a currency other than U.S. currency represents an approximate equivalent to the U.S. currency prize for that level, at that time. Prize winners will have the opportunity of selecting any prize offered for that level; however, the actual non U.S. currency equivalent prize if offered and selected, shall be awarded at the exchange rate existing at 3:00 P.M. New York time on March 31, 1998. A travel prize option, if offered and selected by winner, must be completed within 12 months of selection and is subject to: traveling companion(s) completing and returning of a Release of Liability prior to travel; and hotel and flight accommodations availability. For a current list of all prize options offered within prize levels, send a self-addressed, stamped envelope (WA residents need not affix postage) to: MILLION DOLLAR SWEEPSTAKES Prize Options, P.O. Box 4456, Blair, NE 68009-4456, USA.

6. For a list of prize winners (available after July 31, 1998) send a separate, stamped, self-addressed envelope to: MILLION DOLLAR SWEEPSTAKES Winners, P.O. Box 4459, Blair, NE 68009-4459, USA.

EXTRA BONUS PRIZE DRAWING
NO PURCHASE OR OBLIGATION NECESSARY TO ENTER

7. The Extra Bonus Prize will be awarded in a random drawing to be conducted no later than 5/30/98 from among all entries received. To qualify, entries must be received by 3/31/98 and comply with published directions. Prize ($50,000) is valued in U.S. currency. Prize will be presented in different creative expressions, including various currencies, vehicles, merchandise and travel. Any presentation in a currency other than U.S. currency represents an approximate equivalent to the U.S. currency value at that time. Prize winner will have the opportunity of selecting any prize offered in any presentation of the Extra Bonus Prize Drawing; however, the actual non U.S. currency equivalent prize, if offered and selected by winner, shall be awarded at the exchange rate existing at 3:00 P.M. New York time on March 31, 1998. For a current list of prize options offered, send a self-addressed, stamped envelope (WA residents need not affix postage) to: Extra Bonus Prize Options, P.O. Box 4462, Blair, NE 68009-4462, USA. All eligibility requirements and restrictions of the MILLION DOLLAR SWEEPSTAKES apply. Odds of winning are dependent upon number of eligible entries received. No substitution for prize except as offered. For the name of winner (available after 7/31/98), send a self-addressed, stamped envelope to: Extra Bonus Prize Winner, P.O. Box 4463, Blair, NE 68009-4463, USA.

SWP-H12CF1

'Twas the Night Before New Year's...

And all through the house, everybody was celebrating...except Gina Tarrantino. Ringing in the New Year only brought her overwhelming loneliness more sharply into focus. But at the stroke of midnight a kiss from a sexy stranger changed her life forever. In his arms she found solace and heated passion. But would the morning light turn her Prince Charming into a pumpkin?

Enjoy #618 NEW YEAR'S KNIGHT by Lyn Ellis, available in January 1997.

Five sensuous stories from Temptation about heroes and heroines who share a single sizzling night of love.... And damn the consequences!

As Seen on TV!

Free Gift Offer

With a Free Gift proof-of-purchase
from any Harlequin® book, you can receive
a beautiful cubic zirconia pendant.

This stunning marquise-shaped stone is a genuine cubic
zirconia—accented by an 18" gold tone necklace.
(Approximate retail value $19.95)

Send for yours today...
compliments of ◆HARLEQUIN®

To receive your free gift, a cubic zirconia pendant, send us one original proof-of-purchase, photocopies not accepted, from the back of any Harlequin Romance®, Harlequin Presents®, Harlequin Temptation®, Harlequin Superromance®, Harlequin Intrigue®, Harlequin American Romance®, or Harlequin Historicals® title available in August, September or October at your favorite retail outlet, together with the Free Gift Certificate, plus a check or money order for $1.65 U.S./$2.15 CAN. (do not send cash) to cover postage and handling, payable to Harlequin Free Gift Offer. We will send you the specified gift. Allow 6 to 8 weeks for delivery. Offer good until December 31, 1996, or while quantities last. Offer valid in the U.S. and Canada only.

Free Gift Certificate

Name: _____

Address: _____

City: _____ State/Province: _____ Zip/Postal Code: _____

Mail this certificate, one proof-of-purchase and a check or money order for postage and handling to: HARLEQUIN FREE GIFT OFFER 1996. In the U.S.: 3010 Walden Avenue, P.O. Box 9071, Buffalo NY 14269-9057. In Canada: P.O. Box 604, Fort Erie, Ontario L2Z 5X3.

FREE GIFT OFFER   084-KMFR

ONE PROOF-OF-PURCHASE
To collect your fabulous FREE GIFT, a cubic zirconia pendant, you must include this original proof-of-purchase for each gift with the properly completed Free Gift Certificate.

084-KMFR

Cowboys and babies

Roping, riding and ranching are part of cowboy life.
Diapers, pacifiers and formula are not!

At least, not until three sexy cowboys from three great
states face their greatest challenges and rewards when
confronted with a little bundle of joy.

#617 THE LAST MAN IN MONTANA (January)
#621 THE ONLY MAN IN WYOMING (February)
#625 THE NEXT MAN IN TEXAS (March)

Fan favorite Kristine Rolofson has created a wonderful
miniseries with all the appeal of the great American West
and the men and women who love the land.

Three rugged cowboys, three adorable babies—what
heroine could resist!

Available wherever Harlequin books are sold.

HARLEQUIN®
Temptation

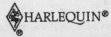

THE COUSINS

Olivia Okrent and her cousins grew up spending their summers at the family's country estate, unaware that dark secrets and haunting betrayals would one day be their legacy.

Now the cousins have lives and families of their own, getting together only for special occasions. But when lies and infidelities threaten her comfortable life, Olivia is faced with a choice that may separate her from her family, once and for all.

by

RONA JAFFE

Available this December at your favorite retail outlet.

 MIRA The brightest star in women's fiction

MRJTC

Look us up on-line at:http://www.romance.net

You're About to Become a *Privileged Woman*

Reap the rewards of fabulous free gifts and benefits with proofs-of-purchase from Harlequin and Silhouette books

Pages & Privileges™

It's our way of thanking you for buying our books at your favorite retail stores.

PROOF OF PURCHASE

HT-PP20

Offer expires March 31, 1997

Pages & Privileges™

**Harlequin and Silhouette—
the most privileged readers in the world!**

For more information about Harlequin and Silhouette's PAGES & PRIVILEGES program call the Pages & Privileges Benefits Desk: 1-503-794-2499

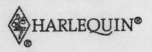

HARLEQUIN®